ALL THE COLORS
IN
BLACK & WHITE

The Oracle Literary Magazine
Bartram Trail High School

Introduction

Today's world is a daunting place, even to adults. So why should it come as a surprise that our young people find it a confusing, challenging, even overwhelming place. Especially now... And yet, this book was written before the darkness of our current times fully had us in its grasp.

For years I have helped young people publish. The challenge given for this particular project was for a group of young writers to deeply ponder and honestly write about the world they were living in. In the process, they explored the diverse faces that make up the fabric of our society and the many problems that they face. It soon turned into a multiyear project as they had a great deal to say. And they had an insight as to where we were headed that was well beyond their years.

As a writer, I have strived to teach them the great power of words. Words can break a heart or mend it. They can start a war or end it. Writing can help us make sense of things that seemingly have no logic. Help us navigate through the darker and more twisted times of our lives and come out the other end. Words can sustain us. And words can heal, whether anyone else reads them or not. But if the words are put out into the world and they are read, they gain a power all their own. For once planted, they can be the seeds of change.

Personally I find it uplifting that our young people can perceive the darker truths of the world, see the great changes that need to be made, and yet still look to the future with hope. May their words enlighten and inspire you.

The Editor: Mary T. Mullen

About the title:

After much thought we chose the title: *All the Colors In Black and White*. We hoped that the reference to all colors would get across our desire to represent a diverse spectrum of faces across different walks of life, each facing their own problems. The reference to "in black and white" was a nod to several things: to the ink and paper, to print newspapers, and to the truth of things, which all good journalists should aspire to. True, we are presenting you with works of fiction. However, throughout history, writers of fiction have drawn inspiration from real life. At their best, they not only entertain, they also provide bits of wisdom that can make the world a better place.

Table of Contents

Homeless

People don't generally plan to be homeless, but it happens. These poems and stories explore the idea that the homeless are no different than anyone else. They sometimes need help, they sometimes need to help themselves, and they sometimes have only the knowledge of what went wrong, and that insight may help you.

Guitar Case

Heather Edgcombe

I'm a star
The corner of Colby and Chase Blvd. is my stage
With a guitar on my knee I bring the passerby a small spark of joy
My hands tremble, my fingertips bleed as they are rubbed raw on the
strings
The smiles of toddlers motivate me to keep going despite the insistent
tugs of their mothers
"Look away, don't encourage him."
Their giggles and shrieks encourage me more than they know

I'm a teenager
The alley behind Vino's Pizza is my bedroom
An old winter coat makes for a makeshift pillow in the summer and a
blanket in the winter
I use my guitar case as a barrier against the drunken wanderers leaving
the Irish pub
Their eyes hold only disgust
But I can see no pedestal holding them any higher
The thought that my parents may one day accept me as I am
motivates me
To leave the damp alley every morning

I'm a human and the world is my home too
I like frozen yogurt with brownie chunks
I listen to way too much 80's pop
I'm a person
Just like my parents, the toddlers, their mothers, the drunken
wanderers,
and everyone else who has walked on this side of Colby Boulevard.

I'm Home

Venetia Lagoutaris

"Good Boy"
he whispers. We watch cars go by
He scratches behind my ears
where I cannot reach
my master
my king
I can do no wrong in his eyes
"Good boy."
I feel my bones wither with age
he pushes me in his metal box
we see the world
we are misfits
I am never less than his
"Good boy."
The people pet me
feed me
love me
but never as much as he does.
He feeds me first
keeps the rain off me.
I cannot feed him
I cannot give him a home
but he is my home,
my good boy.

Saving Grace

Britteny Donor

I stared at the house burning in front of me, disorientated. A woman's scream rang in my ears and I spun wildly to find where the sound came from. I attempted to run around, trying to find her. Although she was nowhere in sight, I knew who she was. But no matter where I ran, I kept ending up in front of the house. I reeled around again as another scream sounded. The blood in my ears pounded louder as the urgency to find her grew. A sense of déjà vu hit me as I began to panic. I looked to the asphalt to find a woman curled on the ground. My eyes began to water, looking at her. She seemed so small, despite being partially sprawled out. I started towards her, arms outstretched until I heard something that pulled at my heart. A baby's cry. I turned back towards the building.

Without hesitation, I rushed inside, bursting through the fiery door. A tearing yell ripped through my lips as a sharp searing pain raked up my arm. I grabbed at the wound, my burning sleeve singing me. I ignored it as another cry seemed to reverberate throughout the house, echoing mine. I gazed up the stairs where the child's room was.

Barely placing my foot onto the first step, the ceiling above fell through, collapsing the stairs and blocking the way up. I wrapped my arms and hands in what remained of my sleeves and pounded against the mix of burning plaster, wood, and drywall. I fell to my knees and the floor surrounding the stairs seemed to fall away into darkness. I was only burning my own hands and with each strike, the mound seemed to grow harder. Chest growing heavy with smoke and anguish, my coughs were simultaneous with the baby's cries. Tears sprung around my eyes once again as I stood in the flames, helpless. The child's sobs turned to howls of pain. The wailing slowly died, and then silence. Another wave of panic hit me in one last desperate attempt as I began to cry. The fire danced around me and hands grabbed me, dragging me towards the darkness below.

I woke with a start, chest heaving. I groaned and grabbed at my heart. These dreams haunted me for yet another night. No, not dreams. Memories. The park bench beneath me no longer felt comfortable nor inviting. I feared returning to sleep anyway. Sitting up, I rubbed my face restlessly. I looked up at the dark trees. Figures seemed to reach up into the never-ending oaks. I scratched my chin through the thick beard growing there. I grabbed the nearly empty bottle beside me, peering inside. I sighed as I found that the beer had been invaded by bugs despite the paper bag around it. I grumbled, more than disheartened that I would need to find a way to get more.

I decided to head to the park's fountain where people constantly threw change into the water. I took off my heavily worn shoes and rolled up the bottoms of my torn pants. I waded into the cool water and ran my hands along the rocky bottom. I pocketed the wet change and when I had collected what I thought was enough for several drinks, I returned to the bench to await for the sunrise.

I sat against the cool stone wall, watching the people of San Francisco pass me. I could feel the gazes of several people. Some of them had pity, others disgust. But most of them kept their gaze averted. Anywhere but on me. I didn't need to be able to read thoughts to know what they thought about me.

Couples passed me often, arm in arm, giggling. Young lovebirds frequented the café I sat across from. It was mostly the women who would go to hand me money until they saw the drink in my hand. I began to hide my drinks to encourage the cash.

"Please," I croaked, "spare change." I just needed enough money to buy another bottle that could keep me warm and stop me from thinking. That was all I required, a couple of drinks to make the nights pass faster.

The worst part was the children. The painful reminder of what I could've had. I often caught myself staring at one of them until their mother pulled them away in fright.

"Mommy, what's wrong with him?"

"What's he doing? Why does he smell so bad?"

"What happened to him daddy?"

"Why is he staring at me? What's wrong with him momma?"

I took a hefty drink from the bottle in my bag as discreetly as I could. A few drops rolled down my chin and past my beard, onto my lap. Tracing a finger along the lines in the sidewalk beneath me, I began humming. A lost man's tune. Lost and pained. Day in and day out, the same thing. Watching faces distort and form into the same ones that haunted me. The sun beating down on me, burning me despite the several layers of clothing. The heat a painful reminder.

I closed my eyes and leaned back, resting my head against the wall, my chest heavy with the weight of the world on my shoulders.

Then I heard that sound again. I whipped my head quickly toward it. A baby's cry. A mother rolled a stroller past me, shushing it.

The child continued crying and I stared wide-eyed after it. The soft sobs morphed into louder, screaming cries. I felt the hands grab me.

"No no no no." I repeated over and over, grabbing my ears. I clenched my eyes shut and tried to block the sound out. No relief. The cries continued and I could feel my heart pounding. I was pulled back into the house despite my attempts to cling to reality. My eyes burst open.

Faces turned into those of demons. Flames sprouted from the cracks in the pavement, changing the burning carpet. The sky darkened and the sun became even more unbearably hot.

I rose to my feet, one hand clutching my head the other grabbing the wall behind me for leverage. Back at the foot of the stairs, I turned to see the woman on the ground again. Stuck in my past, I picked her up and held her, sobbing into the crook of her neck.

After what felt like hours, I suddenly looked up and I had returned to the city, well into the afternoon. I looked down at what once was a woman, and found my bag, tear stained. I dropped it and cupped my face.

I crumpled onto the street, a desperate and tattered mess. I gasped for air and pressed my back against the wall, trying to ground myself. Tears continued streaming down my face as I got back up. I couldn't do it anymore. I couldn't keep living like this. Heaving my duffel onto my back, I moved along the road, letting it take me where it would. More looks from different people, but also all the same. I dragged myself along, waiting for a sign.

Trudging along, I received my sign. I looked up and saw a beautiful sight. The Golden Gate Bridge. A small, crazy smile lifted the corners of my chapped lips as I continued on, purpose filling me for the first time in months. Had it been months? It did not matter. The lights on the orange bridge made it glow a golden color, truly living up to its name. It looked like the door to heaven, or at least an illusion of. I admired the beauty of it; I was always a sucker for pretty things. Another wave of depression washed over me as I recalled the beautiful things I used to have.

Each step up the bridge felt closer and closer to relief, lifting the burden of life off my chest, but the weight of guilt built. My feet dragged along the walkway and what felt like hundreds of cars passed by, all of them oblivious to what was happening. A taxi slowed next to me, window rolled down.

"Yo man, you okay?" the driver called out.

I looked towards him with an elated smile. "Better than I have been in a long time."

"Do you need to get anywhere?"

I laughed hysterically. "Yes, but *you* can't get me there."

He appeared to be alarmed and drove off without a wave.

Laughing again, I watched him speed off.

Once nearing the highest point of the bridge, I dropped my bag to the ground.

One step, I was at my home before it burnt to a crisp. I was arguing with my heavily pregnant wife. My beautiful wife. I remembered that day, how angry we were. I had driven off after that to a local bar. I knew what I was doing was wrong, but it was supposed to be a one-time thing.

Another step and the middle of the night flashed in my mind. I had snuck out of the house a few weeks later while my wife was sleeping and I was on the couch. My other woman had given me a simple leather necklace with a wooden charm to keep. I came back home and no one was the wiser.

The sound of metal clinking suddenly pulled me from my flashbacks. Dazed, I looked towards it and found a large dog on the opposite side of the bridge. All alone and walking in pace with me. It looked towards me a brief moment before a car blocked my view for all but a second, and it was gone.

I was taken aback before another step brought me back to my past. The happiest day of my life. My child was born and I held my little girl in my arms in that emergency room. My wife smiled at me from the hospital bed and my life was coming back together.

A car honk woke me from the most euphoric part of my memories and I looked down into the dark water below. Well past nightfall, the stars above were beautiful and calling for me to join them. I hoisted myself up onto the opposite side of the railing, hugging the lamp post with one arm. I glanced at my forearm, the painful scar from the night of the fire felt like a fresh wound, serving as a strong reminder. A lump built in the back of my throat as I tugged down my sleeve and shut my eyes.

A last flashback brought me back to what had brought me here. The night of the fire, a year today. I had slipped out of bed with my wife in the middle of the night to the parlor to think about what I had to do. I had used a candle to light my way through the house, hoping not to awaken her or our baby. After a lengthy reflection, I knew I had to cut off my affair. I left the house in haste to meet her, hoping to break things off. She hadn't taken it well as she threw things and vowed that I would never see her again. She cursed my name and threw me out.

That is when I returned home to find a raging fire engulfing my house, the smoke forming an enormous column that reached far into the midnight sky. My dream kicked back in, the running and the helplessness as my child burned in the flames. I had returned outside to hold my wife as she died in my arms.

"Baby, please don't leave me," I had begged her, clutching her tightly. " I am so sorry for everything. This is all my fault."

I knew that I was to blame; that I was the reason that our home was burning. The candle I had lit before I left.

She gasped for breath as she struggled to speak, but no words left her mouth.

She reached up, cupping my face in her hands. I leaned into it. Her now frail hands were black and cold.

"Just know," she coughed in between every sentence, every hack more intense than the last. "I have always known. But I forgive you. I understand. I have always loved you all the same."

She smiled slightly before moving her hand down to grab the leather cord around my neck. She yanked it and the necklace fell into her hands. She tossed it towards the burning house. After a moment, there was nothing left of it. She looked at me and I could see the light disappearing from her eyes.

"I love you so much. " I cried into her. No response. I looked at her again to find that she was gone, despite the presence of her body.

Red and blue lights flashed over us, washing her face in brilliant colors.

I was pulled from my last memory by a bark. I looked to my side to find the dog from earlier staring at me. I wiped the tears from my eyes and shooed it.

"Get out of here." I yelled at it, emotional from the flashbacks.

It barked at me again. I turned back to the water, preparing to jump. It was merely a step away; all I had to do was fall.

Another bark and I turned back to the dog. It was walking away, straight into oncoming traffic.

"No stop!" I cried, swinging back over the railing. The dog halted and looked back towards me, tail wagging. "Come here boy, come here."

It returned to me as I called it, its tongue rolling out of its mouth.

I rubbed its head. "What're you doing out here?"

It gave a woof in response and the corner of my mouth lifted. I looked at the dog carefully. It was particularly boney, its hipbones and ribs prominent. I reached for its tag but the dog lacked a collar. I raised an eyebrow suspiciously.

"No owner huh? I'm sure someone in the Bay Area would be willing to take you." It looked at me, head cocked to the side. " Come on then, I better take you off this bridge before you run into more traffic.

It barked at me again and kept close to my side. I went to pick up my bag from earlier but the dog beat me to it, grabbing it in its mouth and bringing it to me.

I picked it up and slung it over my shoulder. "Good...," I glanced at it from the side. "girl?"

It ran in a circle and looked at me happily. We continued down the bridge together. Once we had reached the bottom, I attempted to shoo it again.

"Go on now, get out of here." It continued to sit at my feet, looking up at me. After several attempts, I gave up.

I continued back to the park benches, the dog tight on my heels. I even tripped over it a couple of times. Once we arrived I laid down, my bag becoming my pillow. The dog laid under the bench, curling up underneath me. It listened attentively to my heavy breathing, its eyes darting all over in a protective manner. I narrowed my eyes at it, finding it strange that this dog had come right at the moment it needed to, merely a step from death.

I still felt just as guilty, but something had changed. I wasn't sure what, but I felt different. As I mulled it over, I drifted off to sleep.

The next morning, I woke up to a wet tongue combing over my face. Heavy daylight streamed through the trees onto us. I pushed the dog off me, wiping my face.

"Gross." I said, wiping the slobber off my face. It looked at me happily. I rolled my eyes and sat up.

I continued about my day, returning to the fountain to collect more change. The dog followed me, not caring what I did. It splashed in the fountain, ran circles around me as I walked, and sat with me alongside the streets.

When I went to one of the grocery stores, it followed me inside. Several employees noticed us but didn't say anything, merely whispered among themselves. Perhaps they felt bad enough for the dog and me that they wouldn't say anything like normal. I continued to the alcohol section to pick up a six pack: a lucky day and someone had a great idea to throw dollar coins into the fountain.

As I picked up the beer, the dog nudged me. I looked at it for a moment before I faltered. The dog's bones clearly stuck out to me, showing how skinny it was. I looked at the six-pack of the beer again. I sighed and placed it back. The dog looked at me curiously, following me towards the pet section. I grabbed a bag of dog food off the shelf and the dog barked happily. I grabbed a chicken from the deli and continued to check out at my usual cashier, a young girl who was always friendly to me.

As I placed my two items on the conveyor, she smiled at me.

"Hey, welcome back! Haven't seen you in a while. "

I returned the smile and rubbed the back of my neck. "Yeah, I didn't have the money."

She nodded understandingly. She looked at the dog and gasped. "Oh my, where did you pick up this adorable fella?" She made adoring faces at the dog over the counter and the dog gave a soft bark.

"It's been following me since yesterday and I can't really get rid of it, no matter what I do." I replied.

"What's its name?" she questioned curiously.

"Um, I'm not sure," I said. "I haven't named it."

"You definitely should! If it doesn't have an owner, it's yours for the keeping!"

"I have no idea what I would name it." I looked at the dog. "I'm not very good at those kinds of things."

"Hmm," she thought. "How about something like, Grace?"

"Why that name?" I pursed my lips.

"It's my best friend's name. Her daddy was a war veteran and he had a bad case of PTSD, but when she was born, he started getting better. And your bud here looks positively like an angel."

I nodded. "Grace it is."

As she scanned my usual items, she looked at me in surprise. "I see you're getting different items from your usual." She grinned approvingly and in that moment from the way she beamed at me, for the first time in a while, I felt as though what I was doing was right. "Alright your total will be…"

I began pulling out coins from my pocket.

She paused a moment before continuing. "Actually, don't worry about it; I'll cover it for you."

She pressed a few buttons and the total on the screen flashed to zero. She looked back at me, still beaming. "Have a nice day sir."

I tipped my head to her. "Thank you so much."

"No problem. Enjoy the rest of your day!"

As I walked outside with the bag of free food in my hand and Grace by my side, things suddenly did not seem so bad.

Not Just Another Joe

Tommy Gravenstein

For every action there is an equal and opposite reaction and so for every dark there is a light.

In the summer I live next to the music shop and in the winter I stay in the shelter. In my days I've seen a lot of things: hardships and good time alike. From what I experienced in the Second World War, I realized that humans will never be perfect, even if they strive towards it. I've been through wars and peace, and day after day I find myself lucky to be where I am.

There's a lot of bad in this world: starvation, violence, disease, hate, greed, and death. My dad used to say that dark times bring dark moods and I've seen quite a bit of that. People passing those in need, not sparing a minute to help out.

But I believe in humanity and I believe in the kindness of people. I believe that even though we might not be able to see anything good in our life just now, there is still good to come from everyone and everything in it. It's not the end. It's never the end, if something is left undone or unsaid, and just because I might not have everything I envisioned once, it doesn't mean I don't have time left to get to that.

People see homelessness as a curse. I see it as a way to look at the world from a different angle. One that provides perspective on what I can do to better myself and what I can do to better everything around me. I have faith in life and I know it will be kind to me. I think that's the secret to life, ya know? Just keep hoping.

My name is Joe.

Author's Note:

My inspiration for this piece was a conversation I had with a homeless man in Philadelphia who told me to always look at the bright side of life. He talked about how there is always a silver lining in any situation, and that even though he was in a bad spot, he believed in the goodness of the universe.

Lessons In How To Succeed In Business
With Your Life In Your Pockets

Malea Jones

No one cares if you do your hair in the gas station bathroom.
In a pinch, a hair iron will suffice in place of a real one.
Three shortbread cookies from the break room and a cup of
coffee has enough calories to replace dinner.
When three shortbread cookies and a cup of coffee will not do,
Brian keeps beef jerky in his desk drawer. You'll thank him,
someday.
Staples are sturdier than stitches, just hope you never tear
anything more than your pant leg.
Sleeping at your desk will earn you overtime, just set your alarm
at intervals.
Be careful near the paper shredder, your insurance package
won't renew for another week.
Paychecks are slower than overtime minutes here, hold your
hands over your stomach at night and breathe, breathe away the
hunger.
Purell will clean sharpie from the folders you found behind the
Staples store.
There are approximately 5,036 calories in a travel tube of
toothpaste; savor them and it will almost feel like nourishment.
A jar of peanut butter can last for five months, if you pace it,
and a year, if you agonize over it.
Fold your blazer when you sleep, the pressure of your back on
the bus bench is nearly enough to press it straight.
Take notes, write down everything you hear and learn and see,
and one day you will be able to hold hunger at an arm's length,
to sleep soundly on a schedule all your own.

Georgia

Katie Williams

"Amelia! Where is your coat?" Mother screeched in a panicked voice that could have been heard in the next-door-neighbor's house.

"I don't know mom, I had it yesterday." Amelia, confused, started to help her mother look for the lost article. Now this is strange, she thought to herself, *I didn't leave it at school did I? That couldn't be possible because I remember setting it out by my backpack the other day.*
She stood up suddenly remembering where it could be. "Mom I think I left it in the kitchen. I'm going to go check."

"Okay, tell me if you find it," mother replied somewhat doubtfully, still rummaging through drawers and cubbies hoping that it would soon turn up. As Amelia ran out of the room to retrieve her coat, a tired Franklin slinked in partially hiding in the doorway.

"Mommy?" he almost whispered.

"What is it baby?" mother said, as she was slowly realized that it was not only the winter coat that was missing.

"I know where Amelia's jacket is," Franklin mumbled, shrinking further into the doorframe.

She stopped digging, "Well could you please tell me? We are starting to run late here bud, and it's twenty degrees outside."

"Mommy," was all he could muster.

"Where is the jacket, Franklin?" her voice now becoming more stern.

He tried to look anywhere but at his mother, but her expectant glare reeled him in and coaxed out his answer, "I have a friend at school, her name is Georgia and she is always cold. Georgia told me how they used to go surfing but now they're camping. I wanted to make she is warm because its chilly and she is a girl so I gave her Amee's girl jacket."

"Surfing? Camping? Franklin what are you talking about? We live in Ohio. Oh my goodness, Franklin do you mean couch surfing?"

"Yes! Georgia and her mommy go couch surfing all the time!" the boy seemed excited at her realization.

"Sweetie, does Georgia have a place to live?" she asked inquiring of the small child.

"No mommy." he started to whisper again.

"Sweetie, how about I drive you to school today and we drop off some things for Georgia, and her mommy?" she asked.

"What about Amelia, won't she be cold too?"

"That's okay pumpkin, she can borrow my jacket." She bent down and hugged her son as hard as she could, realizing what he had done.

After driving the children to school, the mother leaned back in her seat and took in a large sigh. What was she going to do? Her amazing little boy. He knew of this little girl and her mother and he decided to help them. No one watching. No one telling him what he needed to do. This poor girl and her mother; she knew what she needed to do.

As she waited in line to pick up the children from school, she scoured the sea of children, looking for one that might be Georgia. Kids climbed into the car just as she saw a woman ushering away a little girl wearing Amelia's winter coat. She threw the car into park and ran after them. Stopping only seconds away from running into both of them. She looked at the mother of Georgia and with hopeful eye, "Hello, my name is Cathryn and I would like you two to come and stay with us in our home. It's cold outside and you both need to keep warm." Georgia's mother broke down into tears and let Cathryn lead her back to the warmth of the family car.

Things are Looking Up

Zan Harris

William's eyes opened, revealing his baby blues to the dull city environment around him, which was the dirty alleyway he called home. Last night, he had completely cleansed it of all the trash he could find so he could safely put down his sleeping blankets. Sadly, however, that did not include many of the weird stains that permeated the walls and ground. His alley may have been a scummy, concrete alley, but it was his, so it'd better be clean...ish. Actually, to be precise, it wasn't entirely *his* alleyway. The blankets that *were* his had gone missing. *Dammit.*

William's compatriot rose, the guy who shared the alley, and with a lazy smile on his face staggered over to William.

"Hey there, buddy. How was your night?" His smile remained, and his breath reminded William of Bourbon Street an hour or so after Cinco De Mayo.

"My night was understandably cold. Can you guess why?" William raised a seemingly angry eyebrow and awaited the response of his boozed up buddy, who had just begun rifling around in his pockets for something. The answer to William's question never came, so he asked another. "Why are you so drunk this early in the morning?"

"Drunk? I'm not drunk," he replied, obviously drunk out of his wits. The stumble, the slight slur, all of it was telling William that...*yeah, he was pretty drunk.*

"Okay, yeah, and my name isn't William!" He sighed and looked to where his friend, Lazarus, had been sleeping, and there he found his missing blankets. *All* of his blankets. It made him understandably upset, but not to the point where he would cause trouble over a couple of taken blankets.

Lazarus extracted a small, white carton of what William knew as cancer sticks--or, as the common-folk call them, cigarettes--and he proceeded to fish out another object from one of the many pouches and pockets he managed to cram onto his person. A feat which William considered supernatural. Lazarus ended up extracting a small lighter as well, his eyes now falling upon his dear friend William. "Want one?"

William shook his head, gathering up his blankets and stuffing them in his backpack, which he slung onto his back moments later. "You know I don't like smoking."

"Alright, then, uh...what're we doing today?" Lazarus flicked the tiny disposable lighter on, the small yet warm flame igniting the end of his cigarette, which he had plopped into his mouth moments before. A thin line of smoke began rising from it. "I'm running out of money." He took a drag on the cig, and blew the smoke away from William.

Of course you are, thought William.

"Actually, Will," began Lazarus, "could you spare an old pal like me some money? I'll pay you back, promise." He flashed a toothy grin, his teeth yellowed, the gaps in his smile revealing his habit-induced dental hygiene.

"What're you gonna use it for?" William stared Lazarus in the eyes, who seemed to think for a moment before replying.

"None of your business," he gruffly answered, stuffing the lighter and carton of cigs back to where they belonged.

"That's what I thought." William then turned away, and he felt Lazarus' hand on his shoulder before he could even start moving off.

"Wait a second, Will," he blurted.

"What?" Will impatiently responded as he turned back to Lazarus, staring blankly into his eyes.

He paused before speaking, hesitation clear in his voice as the words slipped from his chapped, unsightly lips. "I'm...gonna use it on cigarettes and whiskey," he quietly answered, taking a deep breath.

William let out an audible sigh, his expression falling flat. He met his friend's gaze and spoke with a tone that sounded almost sad.

"Lazarus...you need to get help."

Lazarus stared for a moment and he averted his gaze, his hand falling from William's shoulder. He began to walk away, his voice quieter than it had been before, a slight grumble present in the undertones of his remark. "If you won't help me, then I'll find somebody else. I don't need you anyway."

Lazarus stood on the corner of 3rd and 8th avenue, a flimsy, cardboard sign written on in shakily scrawled marker, the words aimed towards pedestrians who were passing by him.

HOMELESS, IN NEED OF MONEY TO HELP KIDS. RETIRED VETERAN OF ARMY. ANYTHING HELPS.

He stared at the sidewalk below him, his act at the ready in case anybody asked about his past, the aching of his heels making him want to sit down instead, which he eventually did. He did this most days, just sit there with William--who had bailed on him like any good friend would--and hope that people would be kind to him and shed some money from their fat wallets. *Ugh*, he thought, *come on people. Just come over and pay me already, I got things to buy*. He searched his person yet again and pulled out his carton of cigarettes, somebody coming up to him and placing a lonely bill in the old, worn-out cap that he used to collect money from any passers by who were too kind or too stupid to waste their hard-earned cash on him. "Thanks, sucker," he grumbled quietly.

He didn't bother to look up to see who paid him some mind, and he placed a cigarette in his mouth, lighting it just like the cig he had lit up just hours before. He gazed down into the carton, and he felt a pang of sadness. He was out of smokes. He crumpled up the box and bitterly tossed it to the side, a long, weary sigh escaping him. *I wonder where William went?* He thought, turning his head up a bit as he pondered William's whereabouts. "He always was talking about getting a job...lucky piece of...nobody would take me if they could see my history." The corner of his mouth turned upward in the slightest as he reached into yet another one of his pockets, withdrawing a small orange bottle with a couple of featureless, white pills left inside, the label for the medication having been ripped off a long time ago. He stared blankly at them before he gingerly placed the container back into his pocket. "No."

William stood among a crowd of homeless people--people just like him--avoiding those who were sickly and overly disgusting, despite his own condition. He badly needed a shower and to see if he could find a job today. *I've had enough of him weaseling money off 'a me,* he thought to himself, *I ain't gonna stand for it anymore, it's stupid.* He walked to the back of a long line for the showers and waited, his want for cleanliness and--despite how improbable it was--a crisp business suit, heavy on his mind. He chuckled and shook his head at his own outlandish thoughts.

Nobody in their right mind would give up a suit to a dumpster fire of a homeless guy like me. The best I can really hope for is a position at that fast food place, or maybe that tiny coffee shop down the road. He considered his options silently as he stared at his worn, dirty, and unkempt hands, and he huffed, trying to rouse himself. He had too few options ahead, but no matter which of the limited paths he chose, he wouldn't let it slip pass him. "Not anymore, and certainly not again."

Eventually, it was his turn. He took a brief shower, smiling softly at the hot water and privacy the stall afforded him, and he stepped out afterward with a towel around his thin waist. He looked to his old pair of clothes, and he felt like the worn rags wouldn't serve him well for this excursion to the great, terrifying world known as the job market. He had an extra change of clothes--albeit a dirty change of clothes that he probably couldn't wash and certainly wouldn't wear for long--so he put those on before returning to the main room of the shelter. "I'm not opening myself up to whatever freaks might be hanging around here, especially during the winter," he muttered to himself. He walked to the end of a line which was going to a window made of reinforced glass, and, when it was his turn, he submitted a small slip of paper he kept in his pocket. He requested a new (and clean) set of standard street clothes; a t-shirt and jeans, which they gave to him without much trouble. He looked to the clothes in his hands and smiled. "Perfect," he said to himself as he walked off to another private place where he changed into these new clothes. After, he stepped off to begin his search for employment, determination clear-set on his face and permeating his stride. He stepped along the street, a hand in his new jean's pocket and tightly wrapped around a crumpled five-dollar bill which he had saved for this moment.

He walked to the corner of 3rd and 8th avenue, which was a stop along the way to the coffee shop, his eyes locked with the cap of a homeless beggar on the street as he withdrew his hand and dropped the bill inside. He watched for a moment as the man reached into one of his pockets and pulled a carton of cancer sticks out, not even glancing up to Will. William shook his head once more and went on, his eyes once more set firmly ahead.

Decisions

Kalis Figueroa

I often find the smallest of decisions produce the most profound impacts on life. Had I not decided to sit next to the smartest person in my math class, I might not have married. If many years ago, my wife hadn't hesitated at a toy store on our walk, to peek at a beautiful dollhouse, I may not have had a child.

Perhaps on the midweek date night we shared, had I listened to her pleading confessions instead of staring at a waitress, I wouldn't have acquired a taste for more, for excess. If the gluttony didn't cause me to stop coming home every couple nights for dinner, to go out and live a life I thought I missed, my introduction to the euphoric ghosts, the ones whose presence I craved and brought havoc in my life, would've never happened. Every day I chose artificial happiness over my family, my gifts, my possessions, and my life.

There was never a monumental choice, it was the likes of not going to my daughter's recital, which in the universe, may not cause galaxies to collide, but in my world it caused my daughter to stop hugging me when she saw me. Her smiles were frail. My wife stopped loving me, maybe long before, but the first time I noticed was when she looked at me and with a stony expression stated the date. April 5th, our anniversary. I forgot.

For three years I lost myself; I was an addict, and that cost me everything. I was alone with nothing and no one. And maybe I am a man who attempts to find reason and patterns in that which it does not exist. But as a man who has lived life full of gain and loss – I can tell you that if more thought was put into your everyday fleeting decisions, it could save you a lifetime of pain.

Author's note:
This piece was based on an interview with an addict who was an educated family man, who didn't make the best decisions at time. He wanted to give a new face to drug addicts, and point out how it is an everyday thing.

Family

All our lives revolve around family. Whether it is the one we are born with, friends and loved ones that fill that role, or the broken remnants of what was once a home. All these things can shape our lives and who we are. The following pieces will explore the ideas that those that we hold close are often flawed and fragile. That no one can cause us pain or sustain us like family. While we strive for that idyllic family, it takes hard work, and sometimes even harder decisions, to keep our lives going in the right direction.

Christmas

Lucie Horton

The door slams open
She runs down the stairs hurriedly
Christmas, the best time of year
She rips open her first present
Everyone applauds
Her parents laugh
Her grandparents smile
They're happy

The door opens
She skips down the stairs, excited
Christmas, a great time of year
She neatly unwraps a present
She giggles
Her parents watch
Her grandparents aren't around
But they're content

The door creaks open
She quickly walks down the stairs
Christmas, a good time of year
She opens a gift
She smiles
Her mom sits beside her
Her dad can't make it this year
But they're alright

The door wasn't even closed
She shuffles down the stairs
Christmas, a time of year
She opens the one gift there
She flashes a quick grin
Her mom is in the other room
Her dad doesn't make it that year either
But they're okay

The door doesn't open
She lies in bed
Christmas, the worst time of year
She doesn't have any gifts to open
A tear rolls down her face
Her mom didn't come home last night
Her dad left them for good
And she's not okay

World War You

JC Holt

Home symbolizes war;
The tearing apart of sanctum-
Retreating to bedrooms, to kitchens, to couches.
Little ears pressed to doors-
"Mommy, what's a bitch?"

***

Drunken fathers, weeping mothers,
Trenches dug in living rooms
Grenades full of words
"Good-for-nothing, worthless, helpless, hopeless
Cannons shooting hate, anger, torture.

***

Biochemical warfare in the bedroom,
Toxic gas and "I-love-you"
Leave you wondering if it's really your fault
Hiding bruises behind barricades fashioned of makeup,
Masking the pain of "I'm sorry."

Your Ignorance, My Bliss

Madeline Lower

I used to crave it
That absolute silence
This calm place
Inside the madness
Of my reality

I wanted silence
I got silence
It was peaceful
It was what I wanted
I didn't know the cost

I felt oblivious
To the outside madness
If I learned what had happened
My peace would crack
Piece by piece

I learned a bit
I was taught about
The monsters I used to love
They weren't always monsters
They were my family

I learned more
I was taught about
Hatred for the lies
The lies that were my life
The lies that were happy truths

I learned too much
I discovered myself
Who I was, now
That I knew everything
My happy life, now dark

The silence I craved
Took everything from me
It built me this utopia
But just an illusion
It shattered around me

It was gone
It left me numb
It left me angry
It left me alone
It left me broken beyond repair

How could something I craved
Desperately
Bring me joy
Then leave me broken?
How does something I love
Break me?

My peaceful utopia
My happiness
My shield
My salvation
My executioner

It brought me to the brink
It brought me to my end
I struggled against it
I tried to fight
I tried to get away

I wasn't strong enough
I wasn't smart enough
I wasn't able
It won in the end
It was the victor

It was the almighty
I was just a scream
Trying to break the silence
No one heard me scream
No one saw me fight

Can you see me now?
Can you see my struggle?
Can you see my scars?
Can you hear me scream?
Can you see what you've done?

Your Children

Rowan Hall

Do you lecture your children
On how to sit, to stand, to sound
How can you sleep at night
After pushing them into the ground

Do you teach your sons
That strength is the only thing that matters
Your daughters are made to sit blankly
To only sit and chatter

Do you hit your boys
Just because they shed a tear
Can't you see he's fighting a battle
That no one else can hear

Do you tell your girls
It's most important to be thin
But criticize when she hurts herself
There is no way to win

Do you call them stupid
A worthless, broken mistake
You only see the surface
But you sentenced them to their fate

In the end do you really believe
What you've done was for the best
Everything you put them through
Just to be like all the rest?

Christmas Tree

Nia Howard

"Come here, my child," my mother said quietly. She was sitting on the couch, staring at our Christmas tree.

"What is it mom?" I asked.

"Have I ever told you about where I was on Christmas Eve at your age?"

"No, I don't think so."

"Sit, let me tell you."

"It was cold, even for Chicago. It was the type of cold that shook your bones, that froze your blood. It gave you chills, no matter how many layers you wore."

"I'd been traveling a long way, just myself, when I was only 14. My mom said she didn't love me no more, and my papa was never home. She threw me out, darling, she just threw out her own flesh and blood," she said, her voice trailing off.

"How does someone do something like that?" I tried to imagine my mom throwing me out, and it made my chest ache.

"I don't know baby. I don't know. Anyway, I had been walking all day and all night; I must have traveled 22 miles by the end. The tip of my nose was so icy, you probably could have gone skiing on it, and I tried hard not to cry, because it would have just made me colder. I saw dozens of families, all happy and joyous. It left me empty. I felt like someone punched a hole in my chest."

"I came across this big, scary house. It was tall, and cast a shadow over the whole street. None of the street lamps dared to block that house's shadow. It terrified me, and yet something called me to that house. It had a single light on, and it called to me like a moth to a flame. A woman came out then, and she saw me. She saw me and said, "Child, what are you doing out here? You'll freeze your little tail off, come in.""

"Of course I went in, I wasn't going to turn down a bed for the night. She told me her name was Karen. She said "Mind the mess, my child, but come in and make yourself at home."
"I walked in and it looked like a tornado sauntered in, and wrecked everything. There were pillows torn, and broken floorboards, the wallpaper was peeling like old skin. A coffee table, at least a hundred years old, was on its side."

"I almost left, I thought I should just go home, go back and live the life I had, because it was better than this, better than living in some dirty halfway house on Christmas Eve, but then I saw something. Something that gave me a little more hope than I had before I walked in. It was a Christmas tree. It was the saddest Christmas tree ever, it was more branch than bush, most of the lights were out, and the ornaments on the little tips were broken or dingy. But it was there. Despite everything it had obviously been through, it was there," she sobbed. I had never seen my mother cry before, but I could tell it wasn't a sad crying.

I then understood why she loved the Charlie Brown Christmas Tree special so much.

"Karen then tapped me on the shoulder, I hadn't even noticed she left. She handed me a little gift bag.

"I see the pain in your eyes, child, too much pain for someone so young. I know you won't stay here, so I put together a little bag for when you go on your way."

"I can't even remember what was in the bag, but I remember the smile she had on her face, and the joy I felt. "Thank you." I said."

"I left that place, on New Years Day. I felt I could skip halfway around the world. That was the year my life changed. It was the year I met my best friend, your uncle Aaron, the year I went back to school, the year I was adopted by your grandmother."

"When I tell you that I never had anything else, that I have all I want, I mean it. I have your father, I have you. It's all I need."

"Thank you, Mom." I said, not knowing what else to say. "Thank you for telling me your story."

Hidden in the Folds

Raven Vanover

A light shined onto the darkness bringing attention to a young child; his peacefulness, innocence, and vulnerability radiated off of him. Shadows started to form. "*Food...*" the Shadows whispered, over and over again. At first the child seemed to ignore it. The whispering only got louder and louder, the different voices seemed to overlap; faster and faster they got. The child started knawing at his hand.

"Where's his parents?" a gentle voiced asked.

"I'm not sure." said a man who seemed to be made of fog. Seconds passed. Seconds turned to minutes. The man watched the child knaw away at the skin. Time was faster here, in a matter of minutes the already skinny child wasted away to nothing. Suddenly, a gust of wind blew the child away like the leftover ash on the end of a cigarette. The foggy man started to walk away.

"What's next?" the gentle voice asked. "Grayson?"

Grayson stayed silent, his feet making indentions in the ground.

-

Grayson seemed to walk for an eternity. When all of a sudden, the world turned upside down and giant walls fell from slits in the sky. The same child was there, but Grayson could barely recognize him.

The young boy emptied his pockets scattering candy bars, chips, cakes, even apples and carrots. "Grayson! Dinner is ready!" a motherly voice echoed, shaking the walls and the floor rippled like water. The young boy panicked and started stuffing away the snacks wherever he could. A loud, rhythmical thump ensued. "Did ya hear me?" the motherly voice said jokingly. The door creaked and a woman in her early 40's entered. "Everything okay?"

"Yeah, sorry I was just washing my hands." The memory of Grayson and Grayson's mom suddenly folded up like a miniscule piece of paper.

"Did she ever find out?"

"I mean, in a way she knew."

"But did she ever catch you in the act?" the gentle voice pushed.

"Not really; she did find out, it just took some time but... I don't know."

The emptiness rumbled and the foundations and walls clashed into each other forming the same room, only difference was it was a pigsty. Grayson's mom walked in with a basket full of clothes. "Ugh this room," she mumbled. She dropped the basket and reluctantly started cleaning. After several minutes of cleaning she lifted a sheet revealing molded snacks and roaches. As she continued to clean and she found more and more.

-

Blocks fell from the sky fitting together perfectly forming a nice, fairly stereotypical living room. Grayson's mom, and a man who could only be Grayson's father, sat patiently waiting. Grayson walked through the door, noticing his parents "You good?" he asked slowly.

"I don't know, you tell me." Grayson's father said.

"What your dad means is we found something in your room that was kinda worrying."

"Why'd you go into my room?" Grayson said dodging the subject.

"That's beside the point Grayson. We feed you enough." Grayson's dad responded.

"That's an invasion of my privacy!"

"Grayson is there something we don't know or something we did wrong?" Grayson's mother asked compassionately.

Grayson groaned as more and more blocks fell creating massive walls that created shadows over the room.

"Just talk to us, that's all were asking. We just want a little communication."

"Yeah, we signed up for this." Grayson's dad joked.

Grayson hesitated, but eventually he cracked and as he spoke blocks fell, muffling everything he said until all that was left was a pile of the massive blocks.

The gentle voice broke through the clashing of the blocks, "You see that. They didn't abandon you then, they won't leave you now; they love you." A large poster board unfolded covering the blocks showing a collage of memories fading as fast as they appeared.

-

"You did good today Grayson." The gentle voice said as Grayson stood up.

"Thanks Dr. Paige." he reached in his pocket grasping a small piece of paper.

"Next week, same time?" Dr. Paige walked Grayson to the door.

"Yeah, just let me throw this away." He held the piece of paper over the trash and stood frozen. Dr. Paige took a hold of the paper and smiled as she looked him in the eyes. He hesitated for a split moment but reluctantly let go.

Repository of Delirium

Danni Waldroup

Her library is scrambled
The deafeningly sweet silence of her breaking,
breaking
I open a book and nothing but the word insanity
is written over and over
I try to fix and shelve the books,
but each time a shake and rumble
knocks them all down once again
Echoes of screams bounce and rattle around me
I run knocking shelves and novels down
Her screams become a background noise
I cover my ears to muffle the noise
I am kneeling and then falling and falling,
more books but no shelves
They're all in a random shuffle
They cover the ground, hiding the floor
She must not be taking her meds
Order is gone and chaos runs rampant
The library is broken
I have failed her
I was supposed to fix her
She was supposed to mend
I was supposed to be her sanity

Abuse

The following poems and stories reveal that extensive web of cracks that run through the human connection. Sadly, abuse touches too many lives in our society, from substance abuse to the inexplicable abuse of each other; and these wrongs can tear us apart. But shining a light on this darkness may help us discover an inner strength we never knew we possessed.

Broken Glass, Lost Battles

Geethika Kataru

I saw the hand make contact with the side of my head from my peripheral vision before I even felt it. My gasp got lost in the loud creaking and groaning of the garage door opening. My vision was blurry. I felt my cheek, my temple hurt. My glasses weren't on my face. *Where were my glasses? What did I say wrong this time?*

I felt his voice hitting my ears but I couldn't make out the syllables. My head hurt. My temple hurt. I needed to find my glasses.

My sister was crying in the back seat, as the car eased carefully in the garage. Maybe it was my mother. I couldn't tell the difference. Usually my mom cried with loud, quick sniffles and few tears. As if she was trying to hide the fact that she was crying, but moments of weakness made her nose run and her chest heave without her control. My sister cried with wails, like she was trying to prove something. But I couldn't tell the difference. My glasses were gone and my head hurt.

I swallowed, trying to wet the back of my throat, unbuckled my seat belt, and grabbed for the door handle, as the car stopped. Habit. Putting one foot in front of the other, without thinking. Going about business. I felt my toe hit something and a loud clatter filled the heavy, warm air of the garage. My glasses.

My fingers fumbled and twitched, as if they weren't entirely convinced that they should pick up those glasses. Wondering if they deserved them. *Would my hesitation make him more mad? Would he think I was stalling?*

His jaw was clenched, his hands were steady and sure as he creaked open the door to the house. My temple had been his target, nothing more. His driving hadn't even wavered while we were still on the street, the car never swerved. I used to be so jealous of his single-minded determination.

My glasses were cracked as I shoved them onto my nose and walked into the kitchen. Quickly, fingers dragging along the walls. Grounding myself, it felt like my head was stuffed with helium. Nobody turned on the other lights, leaving the house in semi-darkness. The white lights fragmented from behind my broken lens. I clenched the cold countertops with my fingers and waited, watching my fingers turn white. Stark white, corpse-like.

He always had something to say. It was almost like he couldn't control his words, snakes slithering from between his teeth. But I knew better, I knew he meant every word he said. Everything was routine, general. An outburst, a tantrum, nothing more. My hands started to shake and I clenched the countertops harder, my fingerprints engraved into the granite.

I felt light weight in the heavy silence; I forgot to breathe. My chest was shaking. I couldn't even feel the tears that I knew must have been streaming down my face.

I didn't dare make eye contact. Wild dogs take that as a dare. So, I waited. It was because I had something to say, he said. It was because I could never learn to keep my mouth shut, he said. It was because in third grade you would talk over your teacher and ten years later you talk over your father, he said. He came here, he got a good job, he raised me to be successful, he said.

And I couldn't be successful if my chin was in the air and if my hair was cut short and left loose and if my feelings were hung out in the open air to rot, he said.

With every word, I could feel the steps he took towards me like rocks piling on my shoulders. But I refused to fall to my knees and beg. My back hurt from standing so straight and I didn't even notice when my mother had to place her foot in between ours, like she was stopping a door from slamming shut. Her hands were held up in a position of surrender, her back towards me, her eyes pinning my father to where he stood, his fingers twitching towards my face.

You always let others finish your battles, he said.

A Pledge of Innocence

Jenna Ross

It starts with love
First it's the flowers
Then it's the fancy dates
Getting all dressed up
Putting on beautiful makeup
Just to end up with it streaming down your face
You beg for it to stop
When it finally does,
You just lay there
Numb.

The next morning he comes in
He's much happier and has breakfast
You think to yourself,
Maybe he's changed,
Maybe today will be different
As the day goes on,
He stays happy,
And so do you.

Tonight he makes dinner
He brings it to the table,
Along with the alcohol...
You can smell the stench of his breath
From across the table
You eat in silence
As you go to get up,
He snaps...
He grabs you and starts to hit
Punch after punch after punch...

It's the morning
He's no where to be found
You take this as a chance to get out
You grab a suitcase and throw your clothes in
He opens the door with new clothes for you
Once he sees you all packed,
He starts screaming
Within minutes, your world darkens.

It starts with love
First it's the flowers
Then the fancy dates
But it ends in pain
First it's the bruises
Then it's the blood

Heed my warning
Hurry,
Before he comes back
Get out now,
While you still can...

No means No

Kendall Burdsall

Every day I walk outside in fear
That a predator lies in wait somewhere near
feigns being a friend but ends up a foe
that person doesn't get the concept that
No means No.

Her family will question why
their little girl wants to die
A man has caused her to feel great woe
he didn't get the concept that
No means No.

A little boy cries in sorrow
After the first time, he is worried about tomorrow.
He knows no one would believe him though.
She doesn't get the concept that
No means No.

A lot of people wait within a cage
for the world to start a new chapter, to turn the page
The world can change for the better, but it needs to know
the simple concept that
No means No.

The Things that Tear Us Apart

Nia Howard

Part 1: Right Before

It was a relatively cool day for July. I sat on my porch, reading my book and sipping on the milkshake I walked to Burger King for. I could hear my baby brother screaming for joy. I realized that they were getting closer.

"Jordan! Jordan!" he said, running up towards me, breathing heavily. His friends followed close by. "Will you come play hide and seek with us?"

"No Chris, I'm reading."

"Aw, please, please please pleeeeeaaaaaseee?"

"Maybe next time."

There would be no next time.

He left, head down, lip out. I would feel bad if he didn't look like that all the time. Just as I got to the good part, my mother walked outside. "Jordan, what are you doing?"

"Reading."

She stared blankly at me.

"Go play with your brother."

"Why?"

"Because, you're a 12 year old girl and you're sitting on a porch reading. You're supposed to go out and sweat and play."

"I did that yesterday. Look at where it got me." I pointed to the various bruises and cuts on my body. Served me right for playing tackle football with the aggressive 8 year old boys. "Besides if I read two more books for the library, I get two tickets to the state fair."

"Ohhhh so cool." She plucked the book from my hand. "Go play. You can have your book back after dinner." She walked back inside. I could hear the click of the door locking.

Defeated, I join the various children, deciding who was going to be the seeker. My brother was chosen, and we set off. I went and found my favorite hiding spot, one hidden away from even the most clever of seekers. I tucked myself away and pulled out the DS from my pocket. After a while, I hear the rustle of the bushes. *Darrn, so much for my perfect hiding spot.* I looked up. It was not the shadow of my brother.

Part 2: Right After

I don't remember getting home. I don't remember finding the key and walking in. All I remember is suddenly finding myself in the shower. The water was freezing, but I felt like I was set on fire. My muscles were screaming in pain, and my mouth was completely dry. I heard a sudden pounding on the door.

"Jooooooordan!" It's my little brother. "You've been in there forever, are you coming out?"

I turned the shower off, and somehow found a way to move, even though everything told me not to.

"Water's cold." I mumbled, focusing on walking towards my room without screaming. Chris started to complain, but I blocked out his triad as I closed the door to my room. I'm tempted to lock it, but it would raise too many red flags.

For a while, I just lay in bed. The ache didn't go away, yet I'm numb. I can't move my limbs, I can't close my eyes. All I'm left with is...that. Suddenly, I can't think about anything else. I wanted to scream and cry, but my mouth didn't move. I stared at my alarm clock instead. I watched minutes tick by, which eventually turned into hours. It's 7:12:37 before someone walked in.

"Sweetie, it's dinner time." My mom's voice made it into my ears. It felt as if my mouth has been sewn shut, but I forced it open.

"I don't feel so well, so I think I'm going to go to bed."

"Is everything okay? I'll come and check on you later."

"Everything's fine. I think I just spend a little too much time in the sun." I lied.

I don't say anything else as my mom shuts the door. I waited for the creaking sound at the fourth to last step.

Then, I cried. I couldn't help it. First I couldn't cry, now I couldn't stop. Snot bubbles form, like I'm a baby and I couldn't stop. I run out of tears and I begin to dry-heave and hiccup and I couldn't stop. I sobbed for hours, until my stomach hurt more and I passed out.

That night, I dreamt of evil blue eyes, and dying slowly.

Part 3: The Days After

The bruises have faded, but my body still hurt. I felt dirty, no matter how much soap I used and how hot the water was. Baths helped with the pain, but I felt disgusting after. I couldn't leave the house. Not to read, not to play with my brother, not even when my dad asked me to go get the mail. When he forced me to go outside, I had this sudden feeling of panic and despair. I couldn't breathe and I cried on the porch. I start school soon. How am I going to get there if I can't even leave my front porch? I see the way they look at me. With this...knowing look in their eye. How do they know? Did I tell them? Oh, gosh I couldn't even look my own family without freaking out. But their eyes, they burn me.

I started school. I still panic, but I worked around it. I hated my teacher, she had black hair with streaks of grey and...blue eyes. I hated her. I hated the kids. I hated everyone there. I can't hug my mom. She still reach her arms out to me and I couldn't make myself go to her. It hurt me so much when she lowered her arms and walked away. I think she knows. My brother still wants to play hide and seek. I say no. Tell him I have too much homework, that I'm reading, anything to keep him away. I think he's starting to resent me for it.

Part 4: The Months After

I hated myself. It's this deep seeded, dirt covered, mouth-taped-shut kind of hate. I hated looking at myself in the mirror, because all I see is someone weak looking back at me. When I'm alone, there's this darkness that looms over me. My brain goes to bad places. I thought about what would have happened if my brother hadn't asked me to go play with him, if my mother hadn't made me go with him, if I hadn't chosen my hiding spot.

Is this their fault? No, there's no way they could have known this would happen. But who do I blame? I guess, there's only myself.

My family surrounded me, singing happy birthday to me. They placed a brightly covered large cake in front of me. 13 candles stare back at me. I could immediately tell which one the trick candle was.

"And many more!" They finish, jazz hands and all. I chuckled, hoping they know that I appreciated their enthusiasm.

"Happy birthday, baby." My dad says, slapping a heavy hand on my shoulder. I visibly flinched, but make up for it by placing my hand on his.

"Thanks, Dad." It's silent for a half second too long. Crap, I've made it awkward.

"Make a wish! Make a wish!" my brother thankfully screamed, bringing back the happy feeling.

'I wish for the pain to go away' I thought.

Even the trick candle blew out.

I've learned to live with it. The darkness, the emptiness, the wall I've built up around myself. My parents think I'm going through "a phase" but I think it's better that way.

Then, I realized it's been one year.

Suddenly, I feel like I'm back. My body gave out under me, it felt like someone set me on fire. I couldn't breathe. How had so much time passed? Shouldn't I have gotten over this by now? Why does this still loom over me?

"Jordan, can you come downstairs?" Shit, it's my mom. I can't let her see me like this.

"In a second!" I somehow manage to say. "Pull yourself together. Come on, please. Get up. Get up. Get up! Please, please, please."

Eventually, I pulled myself off the floor. It's been 20 minutes since my mom called me downstairs. Where did the time go?

I couldn't live like this much longer.

Part 5: The Years After

There were so many people talking. My parents, the guidance counselor, my principal. There's a sad hum in the room, and it all surrounded me.

"Can you think of anything that might have caused Jordan to react like this?" the guidance counselor asks. Ms. Lewis, I think her name was.

"No, nothing," my mom said. Then, she lowered her voice, as if she didn't want me to hear what she said. I was sitting right next to her. "She's been going through a phase, you know."

The principal chimed in. "Yes, maybe but this was a very serious reaction. We may have to-"

I cut him off. "It's just sad, you know?" Every adult suddenly looked at me, this is the first time I've spoken since we've been in here. "A girl is isolated from her peers because of a misunderstanding. And when she tries to open up to it, to tell someone, no one believes her. I would never want that to happen to me."

"Sweetheart, we just want to know why you stormed out of the class like that. We found you crying in the bathroom."

"I had a bad day is all. I promise." The lie slipped out so easily. "Besides, you can't take *Speak* out of the curriculum because I had a bad reaction."

They all solemnly looked at me. That panicky feeling settled in my stomach. "Well if you're sure..." Some adult says, but I'm not paying attention anymore.

What if that happened to me? I shouldn't tell anyone. I don't want to be called a squealer, be isolated from everyone, and only confide in a weird art teacher. I don't think I could handle that. Before I could get any further into my thoughts, my mom taps me on the shoulder.

"Do you want to go home?" I nod.

As we walked out she said to me, "Are you sure you're okay?"

No, I'm not okay. Something bad happened to me and I don't know how to deal with it. I don't know how to tell you either. I can't control my emotions anymore and I hurt so much, it's a miracle that I get up every day.

"Yeah, I'm okay."

I don't even know how we got here. We were talking about dress code. This is why I hate Socratic seminars. My neck got a tingly feeling. Before I know it, my hand is in the air. Before I can put it down, the teacher called on me.

"Yes Jordan, is there something you would like to say?"

I could feel the entire class's eyes on me, but it was too late. I had to say something. "You guys saying those things is, *literally* the most insensitive thing I've ever heard in my entire life."

The teacher tried to cut me off, but I spoke louder.

"That happened to me. I was twelve. I was playing hide and seek with my baby brother, and someone decided to take advantage of me. Do you think I deserved it?"

The whole room fell silent. Even the teacher stood completely still. Then, the girl that pissed me off started crying. Serves her right.

I couldn't stand to be in the room any more. I grabbed my bag and stormed out. I felt the tears welling up in my eyes, but I fought them back.

No use in crying anymore.

My mom started to cry. My dad looked the angriest I've ever seen him in my whole life. I just sat there.

"When did this happen?" My dad said, one hand tangled with my mom's, the other clutching the blanket nearby.

"When I was twelve."

My mom cried even louder. I wanted to tell her to stop, but this is the first time she's heard about this, so I don't.

"I've been like this ever since."

"So when we came to your school..."

"Yeah, it wasn't just a bad day."

"But why did you wait so long to tell us?"

"I don't know."

But I do. I hated the way you look at me. Those tears that don't even belong to you, but you cried like you don't know what else to do. I never wanted to share my burden with you. It'll never be the same. We'll never be the same.

But, it'll be okay.

My parents asked me questions. I answered them the best I could.

For the first time since it happened, I didn't cry while thinking about it.

<u>Part 1: Right Before</u>

The smell of freshly oiled wood and lavender filled my nose and the warm feeling of my mom's hand kept me calm. The big grandfather clock ticked slowly, and I try and keep my heart rate to its steady beat. One minute to 3. Almost time.

A kind voice charms out. "Jordan, the doctor is ready to see you now."

"I'll be right here waiting for you, okay?"

I follow the receptionist to the back. She brought me to a large room. It also smelled like lavender.

The doctor was sitting in a large chair. We do familiarities, before getting down to the reason why we're here."

"So, Jordan, tell me what happened to you when you were 12."

An Open Road

Katie Williams

Looking back at her life she felt acceptance
But it caused pain
and there weren't enough reasons to stay.
She was smart and strong-willed.
she could see the road ahead all lit up in lantern posts
and see her future, in all ways bright.
No more darkness, no more clutter
No more hiding bumps and bruises.
There was hope, there was light.
She was doing it.
Bravery in her heart drove her forward
Forward into the open.
Forward into freedom.
She did it, she escaped.
Not only for her,
but for the baby right behind her.

Jim Beam

Angelica Parisen

We took Daddy to work every Monday night.
Turns out it was AA because he was in a fight.
He went to California on a trip, that's what they made me think.
Turns out he was behind bars because he had too much to drink.

Mommy and I left home when I was eight.
To see my Daddy, every two weeks I'd have to wait:
the train trip from Jersey to Queens I would take.
Because of Daddy, New York became my favorite state.

When I asked Mommy, "Where are Aunt Lacey and the kids?"
"It's gonna be a while till you know where she is."
I wanted to see my cousin, I thought it wasn't fair.
Little did I know, Daddy got drunk and pushed Lacey down the stairs.

I remember Mother told me the whole truth one day.
All she could say was, "I apologize for the delay".
Ever since I found out he wasn't there the night that I was born,
is when I realized that family dysfunction is our norm.

When Father was taking me home that cursed October night,
he gave me a real reason to be filled with fright.
Seeing him after that day two months later, or maybe it was one,
all I could think was I may be that man's daughter,
but he treated Jim Beam like his son.

Self Image

In today's society, image is given too much importance. Not reality but what people hold as the truth. In a world driven by social media, we are pressured to be the leading actor in a perfect life, to be flawless and happy, to be the person that everyone else envies. If there are imperfections we hide them behind a façade. The following pieces take a peek through the cracks that many of us hide behind. And we question why this is demanded of us.

Self-Evident

Rhys Windorski

Hair pulled back, tight-lipped smiles,
Face full of makeup, elegant dresses.
This is what you wanted,
This isn't what we fought for.
Perfect little acts, always agreeing we're wrong,
Always being put down, always told to shut up.
This makes perfect sense to you,
This makes no sense to us.
We're taught to always be polite, that he actually likes us,
But what do we do when he covers us in bruises?
Men are 'stronger, bolder, smarter, perfect.'
Women are 'weak, cowardly, stupid, flawed.'
Why, for years, are we told lies about ourselves?
Why does our behavior matter, but theirs' rarely do?
Society's played and tricked us.
It's about time we broke out of this cage.
No more tight-lipped smiles, no more covering bruises,
No more being tripped into these scathing pools of lies.
For hundreds of years we've fought for our rights,
And not all of us want knights in shining armor.
This is our time to rise up to their level,
For all humans were created equal.

Perfect Mask

Paige Harris

They announced it on a Monday
in our school's old sweaty halls
that a girl that I had math with
wasn't coming back at all.
You hear the silent questions,
she was perfect to us.
What demons was she fighting,
that we were all too blind to see?
I sat in math that Monday,
beside her now-abandoned desk,
while our teachers warned us not to fail
our fast-approaching test.
I remembered she once whispered,
that she was envious of me.
My parents knew the work it took
just to get a "B".
I wish I'd noticed earlier
or had the decency to ask,
because her world
must have been crumbling
behind her perfect student mask.

This Is What You Did To Me

Mimi Dornford

No longer can I tell,
if I love myself.
You made me like this.
You let me think that it's okay,
to wear makeup in order to think I'm pretty.
Without you it's sunny,
but with you there's a storm.
My confidence is a house of cards,
but you're the one to blow it down.

You made me think that girls like me,
are only cute in a bikini.
But when winter comes,
and it's too cold,
I'm left all alone.
Thinking of what to upload,
on summer's new account.

My pictures include my friends
but I can't really show my face.
If I did,
I'd become less confident,
and soon sit up on the shelf.
Oh the things I did to please you,
and the things I put out for fun.
But in the end you tore me down.
So no matter what I did,
you won.

I put up with your glitches,
and I put up with your cons.
But to think there were pros with you,
Oh the things I could have done.
But in the end all I have to say is,
this is what you did to me.
this is what you made me believe.
But I will believe it no more . . .

Beautiful

Nikk Pless

"Anything that is beautiful, people want to break. And you are beautiful, I'm afraid."
-Ugly, Nicole Dollanganer

"Hey, hey…no, don't cry. It's going to be okay," Twyla said, wiping away a stray tear off Chris's face. "Don't listen to them. Why should their opinions mean anything?"

Chris sniffed and looked up to meet the girl's eyes. In truth, he knew why the football team's opinion mattered. *Because they're right. I'm a freak, and ugly, and gangly, and weird, and…* His train of thought was derailed when Harrison sat down next to him, and planted a kiss on his cheek. He looked at the red-headed boy and smiled softly. Twyla said quietly, "We'll talk about this later."

"Talk about what," Harrison inquired.

"It's not important," the pair responded in unison. Harrison huffed and looked around the stairwell in which the trio was sitting.

"Why do we always sit here," he asked.

"Because," Twyla stated matter-of-factly, "They leave us alone here."

Chris nodded in agreement, and Harrison wrapped an arm around his shoulder.

"Why don't you just let me beat the hell out of them?"

"Because that's not going to fix anything, Harry. Besides," the boy sighed. "I have to deal with this on my own."

The bell rang. They all got up, shouldered their bags, and went their separate ways to class.

***

School was over, finally, and Chris stepped through his front door. He'd learnt to be quiet over the years, so as not to awaken –and anger– his father. The man who had "raised" him was almost always drunk or passed out. Chris hoped he'd die of alcohol poisoning some day. He made his way to the large closet that he called his bedroom, and put his backpack down on the bed. He pulled his slightly-too-large sweater over his head and walked to the full-length mirror he'd found at a yard sale. He looked at himself from different angles and eventually sighed in frustration and flopped down on his bed. *Still fat…as always.*

"JOURNEY CHRISTIAN ROBINSON, YOU BEST GIT YER ASS IN HERE BEFORE I DRAG IT OUT MYSELF AND BEAT YOU!"

Chris cringed at the sound of his father's voice, but obeyed anyway. Pulling his sweater back on, he walked to the living room of the small mobile home and looked at the clearly inebriated man, holding back his look of contempt.

"What, Larry?"

The older man smacked the boy in the side of the head.

"Don't give me no lip, boy. I need a pack of cigarettes."

Chris sighed and said, "Yes sir. I'll be back." *I have to be at work in twenty minutes...* He went back to his room, grabbed his wallet and checked what little cash he had in it, and then left the house heading to the gas station at a light jog.

Chris arrived to work thirty minutes late. He'd needed a shower when he got back from buying cigarettes, and his father had berated him for getting the wrong kind. He was going to be hot in a turtleneck, but at least it would hide the bruises.

"Journey! Where have you been? We've been so busy! If you show up late one more time, I'm gonna have to find a replacement."

"I-I'm really sorry, sir," he stammered to his boss, "It won't happen a-again..."

"Better not. Now get out there. Tables four and seven need cleaning."

After the rush of dinner time, Chris sighed and sat in one of the chairs that hadn't yet been put on a table. He had closed the restaurant alone, and now had the place to himself. He put his head in his hands and sighed. It was then that his stomach decided to growl, reminding him that he hadn't eaten all day, save the singular stick of sugar-free gum he'd made last through all seven periods of the school day. He knew there would be food in the back, and debated with himself on whether he should go investigate. His stomach groaned again, as though coaxing him to go eat. *No, I can't. If I eat, I'll gain...I'm fat enough as it is!* Still his stomach grumbled. *Maybe I'll just go to the kitchen to drink a glass of water... Yeah. That's a good idea.*

Walking into the kitchen, an array of smells hit his nose and he inhaled deeply. Frying grease, cooked meat, and various spices. He was sure it was more his imagination than anything else. But sitting on the counter were various leftovers from dinner. He shook his head and scolded himself. *No! Darn it Chris, keep yourself together. Which would you rather have? A burger and some greasy fries, or the body you've always wanted? Remember why you want to be thin.* Chris exhaled sharply and looked at his phone. There was a text from Harrison. *Harry... Don't you want him to love you?* He ignored the message, this battle was too important and he needed to win. *You don't really want that food, you just want the taste. You fat piece of garbage.* He took a step towards the counter and again set his focus on the food. He should just give in, it's not like he'd lose the weight anyway...

"Fine!" He almost shouted, as though there was someone else in the room trying to convince him to eat. He snatched some food off the counter and sat down on the floor to his meal.

Three burgers and two baskets of fries later, Chris looked down at his bloated stomach in disdain. This was his worst binge yet. Just the thought of the food he'd consumed made him want to gag. He ran to the bathroom and hovered over one of the toilets, shoving two fingers down his throat. He twisted them around a bit until he triggered his gag reflex. His body knew what to do from there. The food came back up. Chris knelt beside the toilet and continued to retch. A few minutes into it, food stopped coming up. He'd done it. He'd purged it all. He cracked a small grin to himself, almost proud of what he'd just done. He cleaned himself up, then the bathroom, then went home.

The next morning at school, Twyla noticed that Chris was being unusually quiet.

"Chris, are you alright? You seem...out of it."

He was slow to answer as he turned his head to look at the caramel-colored eyes and wild dark hair that were so familiar.

"Huh? Oh yeah, I'm alright. I just... I had a really big binge last night."

Twyla heaved a sigh of frustration and Chris began to babble. "I swear, I wasn't gonna eat anything, but someone left food on the counter and it looked so good and my stomach wouldn't stop growling an-"

He was cut short by Twyla's matter-of-fact question.

"Did you purge?"

"Yes..."

"How much?"

"All of it, I think...nothing else would come up."

The girl looked at her friend and shook her head slowly. Chris had been like this since they'd met in eighth grade, but lately his habits had been getting worse.

"Y'know Chris, you've got a lovely smile. Purging's only going to ruin it. Maybe you should stop?"

"I'll stop purging when I can stop eating."

The bell rang and Chris left a very deflated Twyla alone in the hallway.

At home, Chris was lying on his bed, going through all the pictures he'd saved to his phone. *Why are all the thin pictures always girls? Don't people know that guys wanna be thin too?* His phone buzzed then, and he dropped it on his face, startled. He picked up his phone and glanced at it. The text was from Twyla.

<Hey, how are you feeling?>

He took a moment before typing a short response.

<Fine.>

<I'm trying to help you. You need to love yourself more than you do, Chris. We care about you, Harrison and I, and it hurts to see you ruining your body like this.>

Chris sighed, and got up to go to the dirty mirror. He pulled his baggy t-shirt off and looked at himself head on. He turned to the side and sucked in his stomach so it was flatter than before. He relaxed and looked at himself again. *Ruining my body?* He shook his head and grabbed his phone to answer Twyla.

<Harrison doesn't love me. He never did. He just feels bad for me. And I have no clue why you stick around.>

<But that's the thing, he does. He really, really does. He says he can see a future with you. But you need to learn to love yourself before you can accept that. I know because I've been there.>

<What do you mean?>

<Back when I was homeless...I thought there was something wrong with me, and that's why my biological dad didn't stay. I hated myself too. But then I met you guys, and you showed me that there's nothing wrong with me, just quirks that I've come to treasure.>

<Being fat isn't a quirk.>

On the other side of the phone screen, Twyla reeled. She hated when he called himself fat. Her thumbs moved rapidly to respond.

<You're NOT fat. Think about it. You are eight inches taller than me, and only weigh about two or three pounds more. That's scary underweight. Please, if you won't listen to me, listen to Harrison- or get some help! I couldn't bare to see you tubed in some hospital bed.>

Chris read and reread the last sentence of Twlayas text. Tubed in some hospital bed... The words resounded in his head in his head like a warning siren. *Maybe she is right...* His thoughts were interrupted by the door slamming and a car starting up, then fading away. His dad was leaving to go to the bar. *Some TV will help me relax…* He made his way to the living room and turned on their small television. The news was on.

"And later at nine, the eating disorder that ate a girl alive" the woman behind the desk said. The screen displayed a paper thin girl, bones protruding and a tube in her nose. Chris abruptly turned the TV off and got up, shaking. He sped to the bathroom and slammed the door behind him. He turned to face the mirror and slowly removed his shirt. The realization hit him that he was transforming into a skeleton, slowly and painstakingly. The thin fingers of one hand reached to grab the elbow of another, feeling the swollen joint beneath the skin. He raised his arms above his head and looked at his ribs. He counted them silently, *one, two, three…* Was this who he wanted to be?

The next morning was a Saturday, and Chris awoke to clatter coming from the kitchen.

"DARN IT!!"

He knew what his dad was looking for, and he wanted to be gone before he came to ask him to buy some. *Get your own cancer sticks…* He pulled on some clothes, a warm, soft sweater that was well-loved and a black pair of skinny jeans he'd bought, but never worn. They were a little loose on him, but for once, he wasn't proud of the fact. Then he opened the window over his bed, and slid out in silence.

***

He arrived to Twyla's house just as she was waking up. He tapped on her window, and she crossed the room to open it.

"I have a front door, you know."

"You want me to go around?"

She nodded, and with that he made his way to the front door and knocked. Mrs. Jones answered it with a smile.

"Chris! Twyla's just getting dressed, come on in."

He followed the woman inside and the smell of bacon and eggs seemed to wrap around his nostrils.

"Want some breakfast, honey?"

Chris thought for a moment, then saw Twyla at the other end of the kitchen. He grinned and nodded.

"Yes, please!"

Editor's Note, per The National Eating Disorder Association: *Despite the stereotype that eating disorders only occur in women, about one in three struggling with an eating disorder is male.*

Alone

Venetia Lagoutaris

It is a mirror
a mirror with no reflection
Then perhaps
it is a window
but it is no window,
simply a mirror with no one staring back,
no reflection to show
but there is someone on the other side
waiting
desperately searching
for a reflection.

It is a hand
beating and pounding
on the glass
but the mirror does not see
How it can show
that which it does not see?
The mirror does not see tears
the mirror does not see screams
the mirror does not see,
so it does not show.

It is the hand
that moves next
taking up fury
and breaking
the porcelain glass of the spider web mirror
And it is the mirror that remains
long after it has been broken
it is the mirror that takes pity
grief
longing
The mirror of black paper glass
the mirror of bones
that does not see tears
that does not see screams
that will never reflect.

Never What it Seems

Abby Maculuso

They hold hands in the hallway
and he waves to his friends
She looks so happy staring at him,
 but no one knows what's in her head
She cries herself to sleep
and screams until the morning,
because what people see in the hallway
isn't quite so telling.
He yells at her and plays mind games
after he greets her father at the door.
Who knew that dating the high school's sweetheart
would be such a heart-breaking chore?
But every rose
has its deadly thorn,
So she comes into school in long sleeves
dark fingerprints scattered across her arms,
and slits across her wrists,
She smiles and covers her dark thoughts up with laughter,
but no one was aware of what happens after
she comes home from school,
with that bitter boy of hers
He beats her and treats her,
like you have never seen
then takes her out to dinner
like nothing ever happened
So don't let your daughters,
your friends or nieces
live in the shadow of a heartless boy,
because it's not worth anything
to let them be treated like a toy.

Lament of a Heartbreaker

Sam Horton

I should apologize
For all the things I've done
All the things I've said
All the things I haven't
I could, I would, I should
But I won't
I never will
Forever condemned to self loathing
Lying awake at night, wondering
musings of a self aware
Self destructive man, alone
The corruption in my past
Tonight's the recollection of yours
I feel the animosity in the air
The strained dialogue between us
Painful pauses, labored discussion
My mistakes are my own
Out to haunt me
Yet they hurt you most
Part of my past, burnt into me
Soon tissue, burn tissue
I'm sorry.

I'm sorry you'll never hear this.

I'm sorry you're burnt into me.

I'm sorry I'm a memory.

Like A Girl

Madeline Lower

The worst thing you can call someone,
is a girl

Don't cry,
Like a girl would

Don't get so mad
Are you on your period?

Don't cook or clean,
That's a girl's job

Don't dress like that,
Like a girl

You're a man
Act like it

Girls are only prey
Take what you want and leave
Before they get attached

Only the pretty girls matter
If she's ugly or fat,
she's not worth anything

If she's smart or funny,
she won't give you what you need
The dumb ones will do anything

No doesn't mean no
She's totally asking for it
It's not your fault,
Boys will be boys

No!
Why would I ask for this?
How is this my fault?
Why can't you take responsibility?

Being a girl,
Is treated like a sin
It's shameful,
To be a girl

We're girls
Are we not human like men?

We're girls
Can we be smart?
No.

We're girls
Can we be kind?
If you want to be seen as weak.

Should we be dumb?
You'll get taken advantage of.

Should we be cold?
Who will love you?

You treat us like objects,
But we're still supposed to love you

You blame us for your mistakes,
But we can't get angry or upset

You force us into a mold,
But we're supposed to embrace it

You make us take care of you like we're your mother,
But God forbid you lift a finger to help.

You give us no respect,
But we should worship the ground you walk on.

Girls need
a man's approval

But the thing about girls is
We grow up

We aren't girls anymore
We're women

Dismiss a man's approval
Take your "love" and shove it

We can be what we want
Smart, kind, and strong

Stop making excuses for yourself
And be like a girl

Why Society?

Hannah Nierenhausen

Why are women flattened by reality?
pushed away by a society
that feeds us our own flaws?
"Pretty,
pretty,
pretty,
thin and
pretty
perfect and
pretty"

pretty without makeup or hours of getting ready.
I'm pretty without stabbing myself in the eye with mascara or
burning my hands on a curling iron;
without spending dollar after dime on things you
might like.
Why, Society,
do you give me no propriety
over who I want to be?
Why do you insist on shoving
every girl
in a perfect little box
when we're not all going to fit?
"Pretty,
pretty,
pretty,
thin and pretty
perfect and
pretty".
When, Society, will you understand that every girl is
amazing, beautiful, courageous, cunning, unique, smart,
and strong?
Why, Society?
When, Society?

REWRITTEN

Lauren Donalson

The spinning of my computer fan and heat against my thighs became too much to bear. I'd reached my social media breaking-point, and the early morning time on my bedside clock did nothing to deny it. I took a last glance at the news article I'd been reading, finally clicking out of the window. I stared at the home screen of the laptop, where a beautiful sunset painted the desktop, one I wished I could see in the dreary dreams that plagued my nights.

I closed my eyes, remembering how sleep took away the ability to feel time passing. Wishing that, of those few, shut-eye seconds, I could stop feeling time, and slip into the calmness, the heart-rested peace of sleep. It wouldn't happen. I opened my eyes with some regret, ran a hand down my face, and used the other to shut the lid of my laptop.

I picked up a journal from the table at my bedside, holding it tightly for a few moments, before I flipped it open, and pulled the pen from the spine. I wanted a journal like the kind I saw in movies, with brilliant artwork and yellowing pages scrawled over with finely inked cursive. Instead, I held a spiral bound, ninety-nine cent notebook I never used for school, half the pages ripped out in my attempts to start fresh, and create that aforementioned 'perfect notebook.' I tapped the pen against the page, no real intent to write at present. I was just thinking. Imagining, if words were on the page, what would they say? Would it be of love, or hate? Neither. There weren't words on the page, and I knew that I wouldn't be adding any. I flipped back to an older work, one covered in scribbles and attempts to hide the heavily-pressed pencil prints that made up the poem. I hadn't thrown it out. I had to keep it for a reason, for these late nights when nothing more was on my mind than the likes of myself and how I longed for a different late night all together.

I stood up with the journal, and walked across my room. Though it was small, the walk across a cold tile floor, in a space seemingly so suddenly foreign, took quite a long time. I stopped in front of a mirror, one that tilted in any fashion I wished, so I could see myself from every angle possible. I kicked it up a bit, giving myself a view from my toes to my hips. I glanced down at the writing on the page of the notebook, and took a deep breath.

I would no longer rely on an old motivation, so candid and weak, so engrained in my mind; it meant nothing to tell myself I was good enough. The notebook was closed slowly, and dropped upon the floor with a soft slap.

Tonight, I would tell my own, honest as can be, time-slowing, cursive-inked love story.

I looked at myself in the mirror, and leaned forward with the blue-inked pen. Upon my feet, I wrote, "Pigeon-toed." From those words, I drew lines to my knees, and circled my kneecaps, watching the pen sink into the spaces between bones on my thin legs. "Knock-Kneed," I scrawled, a word for each knee.

The pen slowly made its way up my body, and my complaints came easier. "Muffin-topped," I pressed the tip of the pen hard atop my soft skin.

I shut my eyes again. Time needed to slow down; I was going too fast. I opened them, and slipped the mirror up. I saw my painted face, and winced. I had more work to do.

"Barely-breasted," I wrote across my cold chest, shirt having been tossed to the floor to give my pen a clear runway. Up to my neck, I added, "Broad shoulders and bony backed."

I reached my face. The pen touched my cheek, and I finally stopped. I could complain about my face more than any other part of myself, and I wouldn't let myself do it tonight. I clicked the pen shut, and dropped it beside the notebook, my eyes locked upon it for a few seconds.

The most beautiful thing in my life had always been my poetry. Words that could dance, sing, cry, laugh, and fly as high as my mind could carry them.

Poetry could rhyme, or have verse as free as a bird. It came in many shapes, many sizes. It came short, tall, and everything in between. The words people could find to express themselves were never judged harshly. Frankly, they were always picked and prodded, a deeper meaning that everyone could sense, but had not seen, locked deep within.

I could be my own poem. My own perfect notebook, without a single missed pen stroke, uncolored picture, or page unworn. Rather than ripping out an old page of my spiral bound book, I started a new one myself. I looked up at my ceiling fan to place the words, the spinning of the wooden blades giving me a meter.

"Oh, you foolish, knock-kneed, pigeon-toed girl, you should move your feet, and fly.

Small enough to fit in the perfect pairs of heels, just right for dancing.

You curved, wondrous, sweet-hearted girl, your shape matches the writing you so adore.

Letters that glide down upon paper in spirals and bends, never being straight lines that no one would bother to glance upon.

Your shapes make you eye-catching, dazzling, sparkling, even!

With shoulders and a straight back, poised and proper, you carry yourself with more dignity than the alpha lion of his pride.

And to speak of pride, the pride held in your glistening smile, one that puts crow's feet in your eyes despite your age, and lets the sudden colored pencils or your body go to work, shading your cheeks with a pink that can only be described as rose-petal perfection.

You are a work like no other."

And as I finally finished speaking, as my quill pen of words ceased to find ink within itself, I felt a weight leave me, like a book being picked up from the shelf after years of dust-collecting neglect.

I was freed from my first-sight judgments. Instead, I had found the meaning in my poem.

Fat little girl

Kiara Simonsen

It started off as a simple lie. I pushed the steaming food away, claiming I was not hungry. I had felt the lie on my tongue. It lay there with a bittersweet tang. Without the food's warmth, I was instantly cold. My body shivered at my decision, begging for the warmth to be returned. My stomach started to knot, as I glanced at my mother, trying desperately to see what she had to say. But she only continued to stare at her phone, her eyes never once flitting from the bright little screen. She only mumbled the usual, "That's nice dear", which just made my stomach knot more. I quickly got up from the table. My stomach growled, but I ignored it. I'm not hungry, I thought, I'm not hungry. This was not the first time.

I walked out of the kitchen, the fragrance of the food wafting after me, beckoning for me to return. I pushed the thought of food out of my mind, hoping that the hunger would eventually cease.

My bare feet slapped loudly against the cool tile, creating an echo throughout the hallway. As I made my way toward the stairs, each step seemed to pound in my skull, causing me to inwardly flinch. I sulked up the stairs, the echoes seemed to increase around me.

My mind wandered to when I was little. I used to love the way everything echoed in the house. I remember that it had made me feel less… alone. Like someone was there with me when I wandered the house.

But the reality of it was, that I was always alone. My mother was never home, and my father, he was never even in my life.

Now, the only thing that the echoes did, was make me hate myself. Each step I made created an echo and each echo created a deafening pound in my head. The echoes only made me feel like I could not escape the humiliating fact of my weight. Each step I took, in my house, in my school. Anywhere I could hear the faintest of echoes, my mind would ridicule me for what I had let myself become. A Fat. Little. Girl.

I shook the bubbling memories and feelings away, desperate to hold the rising tears in. As I climbed the last few steps and turned down the hallway leading to my room, the echoes seemed to increase further. Echoes. How could I ever mistake those sounds for someone being there? All I had was myself, not that that was any better.

My mind focused on my feet slapping the cool tile, each sound turning painstakingly louder with each step. The sounds pounding against my skull, mocking me. My stomach growled, barely audible over the deafening echoes. *I'm not hungry*, I think harshly. My stomach continued to disagree quietly, as I quickly threw my bedroom door ajar. As soon as my feet crossed onto the rough carpet, the echoes in the hallway grew silent, but my mind still warred with the resounding echoes. I quickly close the door, barely keeping up my composure.

I sat on my bed, bringing my knees and pillow to my face. I screamed into my pillow, trying to fight back my tears. *Stupid echoes*, I thought. Stupid, stupid. After a few minutes, I weakly lifted my head, my pillow soaked with tears. My body shuddered as I attempted a few steadying breaths. I chucked the pillow out of my arms, laughing weakly at how I had muffled my sobs. It's not like my mother would have heard me anyway.

I slowly rose from my bed, my body weak with exhaustion. I took my time walking to my desk, trying to prepare myself for the mirror.

As I sat in the chair I glanced up to my reflection, my brain piecing together what I saw. My black curls were in a tangled, sloppy bun, strays sticking to my damp chubby cheek. My eyes were circled with smears of my mascara, making my blue steel eyes seem brighter. Clearer.

I quickly opened the drawer to my right, rummaging for a spare makeup wipe. I tossed random items from my drawer, annoyed that so much had been jammed in there over time. My gliding fingers slid across a sharp edge, causing me to gasp audibly and jerk my hand to my chest. I glared at the blood dripping down my finger. Paper cut. I quickly looked in the drawer, finding the culprit immediately. Some of my blood was on the edge of an old, crumpled photograph. My finger throbbed as I picked up the photo, my eyes wide.

The picture showed me when I was around six years old. I was sitting in my grandpa's ugly orange armchair, nearly swallowed whole by it. My face was twisted upwards, my mouth the same. I was smiling. I was happy. Tears threatened to rise as I looked at little me. When was the last time I really smiled?

I squinted as I lifted the picture closer, spotting a plate of cookies on the table in front of me. I wore a simple blue dress with my hair tied perfectly back with a blue ribbon. My little frail legs were crossed as elegantly as I could, as I read the book that was on my lap.

The first edition of "Lessons of Etiquette: For Young Girls". My grandmother had insisted that I read the book, promising me a plate of cookies when I finished. Of course, I soon came to read the whole series, just as my grandmother had wanted. She wanted me to be the "perfect little lady", as she put it.

My eyes were drawn back to the drawer, where a second picture lay. I wiped the blood on my fingers onto my skirt and picked up the second photo.

Here, I was twelve, maybe thirteen, years old. I filled up my grandpa's ugly orange armchair now, my thick body was tight with tension, my face scrunched in confusion. Nothing in the photo showed any hint to why I had been confused, but I remember. I will remember why forever.

It was like any usual visit with my grandmother. She would fuss over my after-school appearance, openly disgruntled that I had not fixed my appearance myself. She often scolded me for the first 20 some-odd minutes of my visit, not the least bit concerned if what she said were in any way too harsh. After she was finished fussing, she would have me brew the tea as she gathered the etiquette book that she thought I needed to review for the day. She would ramble on about how I should act, dress, and behave around certain people. She would teach me the harsh realities of the world and she expected me to not speak unless spoken to. Which, with Grandma, or anyone for that matter, meant that I should just never speak. After the tea was gone and all her ramblings ceased, she would usually reward me with 3 cookies. That day had been different.

Instead of the cookies, she gave me a small bowl of assorted veggies. My face had instantly fell, my eyes quickly lost their happy glint. My face contorted in confusion, I looked up at my towering grandmother, who had just taken my picture and looked distinctly pleased at my confusion.

"Grandma," my voice quivered slightly, as I knew that questioning her was immensely rude, but I continued anyway, "where are the cookies?" I cocked my head to the side and widened my eyes, hoping this helped me look sweeter.

"Camy dear," my grandmother's steely voice seemed somewhat sharper, "did you even listen to me today? Honestly, with ears like that you think you would be able to listen better!" she laughed heartily, obviously amusing herself.

"You ought to have noticed the lesson of today.." She paused, probably waiting for an answer. When she saw that I had none to give, she narrowed her eyes and continued, her words increasingly becoming sharper. "*If* you had payed attention *at all*, you would have noticed how I was *trying* to tell you about your eating habits *dear*." She reluctantly added dear, most likely softening up what came next. She tilted her head, eyeing me up and down.

My mind instantly replayed the day. When she was fussing over my appearance, I had thought she said something about how I would need a much larger dress soon and how it must be a miracle sent directly from God that there was no tear in my coat, but I can't quite say for sure. During her ramblings, there had been some comment like, "Camy dear, you are too large to sit in that chair, go get the one at the table in the kitchen." She had also exclaimed in frustration during the middle of the lesson, exclaiming how upset she was about the state of my physical strength. "someone of your size should be able to hold more", or something like that.

I looked up at my grandmother, my face still a bit scrunched in confusion. She only sighed heavily and sat wearily in her purple chair. Her eyes seemed to turn to steel right then.

"Camy, the lesson today was not one that was obvious, because.." she paused her eyes holding mine, "well, because I thought it quite obvious, your unhealthy eating habits and I had thought that your mother had talked to you about it. But, enough is enough. I have been holding my tongue for far too long. Camy, I am going to be blunt, so listen now. You need to start eating better. I mean, you don't want to be a fat little girl, do you?" Her eyes bore into mine, making my cheeks flush warm.

Fat? Was I fat? I had looked down at my body, tears starting to blur my vision as I saw my thighs for the first time. I saw how they seemed to barely fit into the ugly old armchair. I saw my hands for the first time, my ring seeming to threaten to cut off my index finger's circulation. I heard my grandmother talking in the background, something about how being large is only going to be a temporary problem.

Her voice swirled into the back of my mind as I looked at my body for the first time. Images of magazines cluttered my mind's eye. I had never thought much about those magazines, but at that moment, that was all I thought of. I remembered the models, how happy they looked. How the words around them told you all about how to lose weight, how to be healthier, how to be prettier. Those images flashed across my eyes as I remembered the days in school when people laughed when I ran in PE, when I was picked last in games, when I bought extra food at lunch. I hadn't really understood, but at this moment, with my grandma, all the pieces were thrown together. *I'm fat?* I thought. Tears slid down my cheeks. Everything snapped into focus. That was the moment I saw myself for the first time. *I don't want to be a fat little girl, do I?*

My mind snapped back to the present as a bead of blood ran down my arm, a red waving streak left behind on my arm. I quickly got up and cleaned myself up in the bathroom. Discarding the crumpled photos back into the drawer.

Ever since that day at my grandmother's, everything seemed to be in focus. My grandmother and my mother would often repeat the phrase to me, "You do not want to be a fat little girl, do you?" I don't think they quite noticed how many times they said it to me, but I did. I noticed.

I noticed the plates and bowls that I had left scattered around my room. I had quickly cleaned them up, swearing to myself to never eat in my room again. I noticed how many times a week I would have usually eaten dessert, I immediately snuffed out dessert all together. I no longer ate multiple times per day. I limited myself to three meals a day. I followed a variety of different diet plans, workout plans, anything that would help me lose the weight that I had unknowingly gained.

I often scolded myself at my moments of weakness, threatening myself with the phrase that I had grown to repeat daily to myself. "You do not want to be a fat little girl, do you?"

I made sure to cut out any and all sweets, never letting my cravings get a hold over me. *I am not weak*, I thought. I do not need them; I will live without sweets.

Soon, a usual meal plan for me would be an apple for breakfast, oatmeal for lunch and a small salad for dinner. When eating breakfast, when packing lunch, whenever I ate dinner, the phrase haunted me. "You don't want to be a fat little girl, do you?"

I ate less and less, never quite full. It felt like a gaping hole in my stomach, a black hole that would never cease. Then one day I decided that what I was doing was not enough. I had not seen any difference in my physical appearance. I needed to step it up a notch. So I decided to start skipping meals. Maybe, I thought, maybe this is the way to not become a fat little girl. It will work, I thought, *this* is the answer.

At 15, I thought that I had finally conquered my stomach. It no longer cried as much for food. It knew the drill by now. I was in control. I won't feed the fat little girl. She knows she has lost. I won, I thought, I finally won. No one wants to be a fat little girl, I reminded myself.

One day, I noticed that no one around me said the phrase anymore. They had just stopped. I couldn't remember when they had stopped, I guess I had always heard them say it in my mind. I realized that I couldn't pinpoint when they had stopped saying it to me and when my mind had started to do it for them. Maybe because they knew I had it under control; that I knew the phrase by heart already. Maybe, just maybe, what I'm doing is working.

My steps no longer echoed. My body felt light. So did my head. Everything was lighter. But, it was also cold. I was always cold. Always in pain. My head would throb, my heart pound, my body ache. I didn't understand. *What now?* I haven't fed the fat little girl, so..did I do something wrong? Am I supposed to feel like this? Is that how you know that what you're doing is working?

One day, I felt *so* light. *So* light, I felt like I could fly. *I could fly over the fat little girl*, I thought, I could finally leave her behind. That would be great, I thought, she couldn't hurt me anymore. I was so light. Light. Then, everything went black.

I woke up to bright lights. I couldn't see. My eyes strained against the white vibrancy. My vision adjusted a little, but everything was still a bit blurry. I looked around, straining to find someone. I tried to lift my hand to my face to wipe my eyes. It wouldn't move. I looked down at my hand. I tried to move it, but it only shook and lifted slightly in response. Wait, I thought, my hand? It was so small I barely recognized it. It's color was all wrong, almost a lifeless look to it in the harsh lighting.

There was an IV in my arm, my eyes trailed it back to the heart monitor. My heart rate was slow. Unsteady. My ears finally registered the slight beeping of the monitor. My heart rate was weak, the monitor beeping deathly slow. I heard my frail shudder for breath. It came in small shaking gasps. My chest would rise and fall unevenly. My chest. It was -- it was so frail. I could trace every rib with my eyes. I tried to crane my neck to examine my body, but pain throbbed throughout my body. Everything hurt. I was so tired. All I wanted to do was sleep. My eyelids threatened to drop at any given moment, but I needed to stay awake. My voice was raspy, I could barely hear it. I repeatedly tried to call a nurse over. I need to know if I was going to be okay.

After the nurse left, I cried. Or, at least, I tried to cry. My body couldn't produce tears. My shoulders shook as I let out frustrated gasps of breath. *It is all her fault,* my mind burned with quick hatred. *That fat little girl did this to me.* My eyes burned as I let the anger wash through my body. I trembled weakly, my mind screaming profanities at the fat little girl.

Suddenly, my mind went silent. My body froze, rigid at my sudden realization. It hit me hard, stopping me mid-thought. A small gasp escaped my thin, trembling lips. *No*, I thought suddenly, *it's not the fat little girl who did this to me. It was me. I have been the fat little girl that I was afraid of. She, is me.*

My body began to tremble again as I lay on the hospital bed, completely aware of everything I had done to get me here. *It was all my fault. I' m here, because of me. I did this.*

After that day, I ignored the persisting echoes in my mind. I forced myself to stop repeating the phrase to myself. I often cried when I ate, but I forced myself to eat anyway. I continued to eat because I knew that there was nothing wrong with it. Nothing wrong with gaining weight. With having fat. My therapist taught me that just because you have fat, doesn't mean you are fat. That was the new phrase that helped to fight the old phrase.

I gained weight since the hospital. I was glad. I was warm. I was healthy. I knew that I would struggle with the voice in my head, but I knew I could fight it too.

I decided that when I have a daughter of my own, I will be sure to teach her what I had to learn the hard way. She will know that she has someone who she can turn to, someone who will help her through her struggles. I will make sure that she never has to feel like I had felt. I will make sure that she will never have to go through what I went through. I don't want her to ever hear the phrase "You don"t want to be a fat little girl, do you?". And I will make sure, she never will.

Rebirth

Hannah Nierenhausen

I am not the cold from all those nights spent alone
I am the hand to hold as the world falls apart
I am not a fight hidden behind closed doors
I am the light I have been searching for
I am not the force of hurtful words
I am the source of my own happiness
I am the sun moon and stars
I am everything I seek
I am everything I need

Rebirth

Hate

There is a lot of intolerance in the world, yet the one thing we should not tolerate, hate, seems to be everywhere. Everyone seems to have a reason their brand of hate is justified. These pieces explore how horrible it is to be hated, what it does to a person, and what it does to society. Hopefully they will inspire, at least a few souls, to rise above their hate.

There's a Word...

Allen Butler

There's a word that can silence a room
Four letters, utter it in a conversation and your
friendship is doomed
There's a word that's caused too much hate
You're born with it, stuck to it, it'll shape your fate
There's a word that's made countless scars
scars from a whip, across the back and the hip,
of a man condemned to a life so hard
there's a word that defines who we are
From birth, people of my complexion get put on
police radars
There's a word that locks my people behind bars
But we mask our struggle with expensive cars
Get that Bentley, get that Jaguar
Forget how they fight
to make sure you don't become a star
There's a word that separates man,
puts us in boxes, draws boundaries between our lands
There's a word enforced by hatred and greed
It's caused pain and suffering despite us sharing
one blood that we all bleed
There's a word we need to erase
without it we'd have a beautiful future to face
there's a word for which I've grown a distaste
If you haven't guessed it, that word is RACE

Brotherhood

Tyler Danson

With your eyes you condemn
With your lips you seek to frown
Your heart resolves to hate
Your thoughts plot to bring me down

Because of my color
Because of my creed
and yet we are the same
the same color we bleed.

But still, I am strong
I am brave
I am free
But in your hate, that is more
Than you will ever be

Never Again

Jillian Findling

Clink Clank
The sound of a pick on rock
Kids were mining
Adults were building
No laughter could be heard
Not one had a voice

German soldiers lined the fence
Not one in this camp had a defense
The chamber of secrets
Hidden from the world
The fumes of gas
Leaked through the vents

Not one truth breathes . . .
Not one kid knows . . .
What happened to papa?
What happened during the march?
Had the mean men let some go?

The stripes were blue
With a pattern of white
The hair was shaved off
Deep in the night

Dangerous
Evil
These are the lies we are fed
Because according to the bad men
Nothing is more horrid
More evil . . .
Than a Jew.

The Entitled Right

Lorelai Vedvick

With a simple raise of their arm and a laugh,
they mock the deaths of many.
The rebirth of the salute that killed women, children, my own family.
But no one cares do they?
I plead with everyone to stop it, to do SOMETHING!
But they won't.
People get away with it, and i'm sitting here seething.
Nothing is done and it's treated like a joke.
"Just get over it, they don't mean any harm."
"No one's getting hurt!"
"Everyone's entitled to their own opinion!"
But thats wrong.
You are slandering the names and lives of real,
actual people who died
just because of who they were.
No real reason.
Is it still funny?
Would you go to someone's grave and spit on it just because
 it didn't hurt anyone?
These were real people with real stories, and you think
its okay to make some edgy joke?
You disgust me.
Open your eyes and see what you're doing.
How it's wrong.
Adults, stop making excuses for the children.
Let them know it isn't okay.
Because it isn't your right.

DELUGE

Garon "Eden" Shelton

Our rights
Our love
Our strength
Our difficult transition to who we are

This won't be taken away
The ignorance that swallowed this world
is becoming unbearable
The peace we once had
Our rights as living human beings in America
Is about to be tossed right out the window

Humans need
    Love
    Peace
    Acceptance
    Encouragement

Don't spread the hate like mere butter on toast
We dare defend our rights

Our teetering hope
Our hard-earned freedom
Our distant confidence
Our almost-attainable goals

These won't be taken away by hate
I am human
We are all human

You stand tall
but the hate you give
will make you small

we will fight restlessly
protest peacefully
to protect and defend us all
This is what we will do for our rights
I am a human being
We should all be human beings

The March

by
Jaysica Nacionales

I marched up my street with 60 other people, raising my cross up to the sky with each step. My parents walked beside me, their voices unable to be distinguished in the solid, unified voice of my church. I mouthed the words and followed along. My priest led the march, spewing random verses from the Bible. People began to gather along the sidewalks. The sprinkle of Pride flags made me smile.

"I'm glad you're finally yourself, you should come to this more often," my mom said into my ear. I kept the smile up long enough until she looked away, attention once again focused on picking out the "unholy ones" in the crowd and then proceeding to thrust her "God can still save you" poster toward them. My smile fell quickly. I felt sick to my stomach. My feet ached. My will was tired. The unified chanting was like a hammer to the head, pounding itself deeper and deeper into my brain.

"Man with woman, woman with man."

I couldn't take it. Splinters pierced my calloused hands. The cross I was holding was old and shabby. It felt heavy and uncomfortable, to the point where it hurt. Almost like it could tell I wasn't worthy to hold it.

"Man with woman, woman with man."

By now we had walked about two blocks and showed no signs of stopping soon. I was ready for it to be over, but then I saw her. The love of my life, clad in rainbow from head to toe. With the same look of determination that I've grown to love on her face. I couldn't help but smile fondly. I loved how passionate she was about everything.

"Man with woman, woman with man."

My smile died on my lips when she locked eyes with me. I could see the different stages of her reaction. Happiness, turned to surprise, followed by confusion, turned to realization, anger, and then disappointment. The hurt in her eyes felt like a hot iron fist twisting my insides. I tried to call out, but they were lost in the chanting that only seemed to get louder.

"Man with woman, woman with man."

I couldn't stop the tears. Like a dam they broke through, but I kept walking. I kept shooting the cross in the air. The splinters continued to dig themselves deeper into my palms. The hot sun continued to beat down on me. Yet I still walked. I marched down the street away from my happiness.

"Man with woman, woman with man."

I let my fears and inner demons control me. I let my insecurities get the best of me and force myself to lock away the better part of me. I'm a stranger to myself. Sweat ran down my face mixing with my tears, leaving a salty taste on my lips and my throat dry; my mind was slowly crumbling. Bits and pieces of my sanity flaking away and being trampled under the feet of my demons that continued following behind me as we marched, brandishing their signs and crosses. The chanting was ear-splitting, each word was like a lash, confining my urges into the darkest corner of my brain in the hopes that that part of me would disappear.

"Man with woman, woman with man."

I shut my eyes tight, wishing everything and everyone would go away. The hot tears continued to run down my face. The chanting never stopped, but I started my own chant.

"Can't let them know, can't let them know."

Violence

After hate comes violence, yet sometimes violence comes without hate. Sometimes, unfathomably, it even comes with love. It is hard to say which is worse. With mainstream media news so focused on reporting violence, it starts to seem like it is everywhere and everyone. It starts to seem normal, acceptable. It is not. Each year in the US there are less than four violent crimes committed per one thousand people. It is not normal. Yet even this number is unacceptable. Here we look at what violence does to people, to families, to homes, and especially to the innocent.

Why?

Natalia Camacho

Fire alarms rang throughout the hallways as I walked through.
Confusion clouded my head until I heard a "Pop! Pop!"

I froze in the middle of the hallway for a second until reality hit me hard.
I ran through the hallway seeing my fellow peers fallen, succumbed to their wounds.

I found an empty classroom and hid in it. My heart beat wildly as fear consumed me when I heard another "Pop! Pop!"
A whimper escaped my mouth and I immediately covered my mouth with my hand.

After three hours of waiting in fear, a knock was heard on the door.

My eyes widened in fear as I pressed myself in the corner and made myself as small as I can be.
The door opened slowly, letting the light in.
I closed my eyes and waited for the inevitable. I prayed to God to make this end.

A whispered "Hey" was all I heard and I peeked up through my arms.
Tears leaked from my eyes as I saw my savior. He pulled me from my hiding position and lifted me into his arms.

"You're safe" was repeated as I burrowed my head into his neck.
I looked up as he carried me through the school.
My eyes teared up as I saw the fallen.

In a few minutes… he and I just exited the building and he took me to the ambulance to check me out.

Then, I was taken to another building where other peers and staff were waiting for their parents and loved ones to pick them up.

It was hours until someone shouted my name. I blankly stared at the floor. I looked up and saw my parents running toward me, their faces red blotched and tear stained.

They grabbed me and held me in their arms whispering, "I'm so glad you're okay," again and again.

I let myself revel in their warmth and then began to feel tired. My eyes started to close. As I shut my eyes, I thought "Why"?

Child

Laura Mackie

Oh child
Where have you gone?
Where has your innocence fled?
Oh child
Where is the boy
with his marching band toys,
who'd rather play than stay in bed?
Oh child
Where is that glimmer,
why do your eyes seem so much dimmer?
Why act like you're already gone and dead?
Oh child
My lovely child
War was wrought and shots were fired
Wounds were healed and troops expired
Yet you never felt that sort of violent pain
Oh dear child
You are not the same
Oh dear child
You are not the same

Worst Day

Alyssa Herrera

This was the worst day of my life
At 5 AM I woke up
At 8:45 I got to school
At 10 AM we went on lockdown
At 10:15 I hid in the bathroom
At 10:18 I could hear an echoing scream
At 10:23 I could hear gunshots
At 10:30 Someone walked in
At 10:31 they found me
At 10:31 I found a SWAT team
At 10:32 they escorted me out
At 10:34 I saw my best friend
At 10:34 I ran to her
At 10:34 I saw the bullet holes
At 10:34 I tried to stop the bleeding
At 10:34 She stopped breathing
At 10:35 An officer pulled me away
At 10:35 We saw three more people dead
At 10:35 The shooter walked in
At 10:35 The shooter shot
At 10:35 I could feel warm blood dripping
At 10:35 I was pushed to the ground
At 10:35 The SWAT team started shooting
At 10:35 Both an officer and the shooter fell
At 10:36 I was helped up
At 10:36 I was asked if I were okay
At 10:36 I said I was fine
At 10: 36 We left the hall
At 10:37 We passed a classroom with an open door
At 10:37 I saw it was empty
At 10:37 I realized I was crying
At 10:37 We made it out of the school
At 10:38 I was taken to get cleaned up
At 10:38 I noticed someone hurt and alone
At 10:38 They had stopped breathing

At 10:38 I climbed on the gurney
At 10:38 I started CPR
At 10:42 Their heart started again
At 10:42 I looked at the wound
At 10:42 I saw the piece of glass impaling them
At 10:42 The glass had nearly shredded their side
At 10:43 I calmed them down
At 10:43 I held the glass steady
At 10:43 A paramedic came over
At 10:43 They told me to be careful
At 10:43 They told me to hold my hand over the wound
At 10:44 We were put in an ambulance
At 10:55 We made it to the hospital
At 10:56 We were taken to an OR
At 10:57 I took out my hand
At 10:57 I was taken from the OR
At 10:57 I collapsed
At 10:57 They realized I was shot
At 10:57 They told me it hit my rib
At 10:57 I was rushed into surgery
At 11:50 I woke up
At 11:55 A nurse came in
At 11:55 I asked about the casualties
At 11:55 I was told that 20 people were injured
At 11:55 I was told that 15 died
At 11:55 I was told I saved a life
At 11:56 I found out that three of my friends died
At 11:56 I learned that the shooter survived
At 11:56 I started to feel the pain
At 11:56 It was all too much
At 11:56 I realized it would never be the same
Today was the worst day of my life.

The Soldiers in the Field

Garrett Henson

Just yesterday I heard gunshots
bloodshed all over battlefields
men were carrying more than guns
hatred was the only thing found.

Now, I can see a different sight
friends are all up in arms today
but they are not sharing sadness
they're cheering and laughing as one.

They are all from different countries
languages held no barrier
cultures were shared with each other
singing songs I don't understand.

Peace is more than a distant dream,
it can be a reality
even in places torn by war
even in times of dreary hope.

In Country

Kenneth Austin

"Medic! We need a medic!" I heard someone down the hill yell out. I wanted to help, and I started to wonder who needed help. *Could it be John our cook, or Sam the teacher or even James the architect.* These thoughts were distracting, and you couldn't afford to do that. You couldn't think about them. You could only look forward.

"Damn." I muttered, clutching my M16 as I grinded my teeth. *I'm going to make it as far up this hill as possible. Please watch over me God.* I stood back up from the half-fallen tree and scanned the jungle. *Flashes, under the leaves.* I aimed at where the gunfire was coming from, and pulled the trigger. The rifle kicked back into my shoulder, as the bullets left the magazine, and fired in the distance. The flashes stopped, and I could only assume that I got It.

"More are coming down the hill!" I heard someone from my right yell. My head quickly swiveled as I stared at several men who were reclaiming the defenses they had lost.

"N.V.A!" I screamed, turning to fire at the charging enemy. They quickly ducked, and got to cover, avoiding my shots. "Stop moving," I grumbled. *Click* "Reloading!" I yelled, dropping to the ground and replacing my empty mag. *Okay, let's give it another go*, I thought, as I rose back up to my feet, ready to return fire. It was then I heard a shot, a shot much louder than the rest. It was the last thing I could hear as I was launched back. My vision started to blur, and eventually faded to black.

"Why do you have to go, you will die if you go." My mom sobbed, trying to convince me to reconsider.

"It's the law, mom. The draft notice makes that very clear," I explained. *I didn't want this to happen, I didn't want to fight in this war, but what my mom was asking of me was borderline treason.* "And what mom, you want me to run to Canada? To run away like a coward with my tail between my legs?" I asked her, holding my hands behind my head.

"You're willing to do this just so you don't look like a coward? You're not a coward if you don't want to fight in that war, you're smart. Only a madman would be willing fight in a war as brutal as that. Haven't you seen the news? They're hurting innocent people," my mom yelled back, her voice quivering as I saw tears form in her eyes.

"I don't want to fight in this war mom... I'm being forced to. Sure, a lot of people have died, but most people haven't. You shouldn't worry too much, for all you know I might not even have to fight. They always need their cooks and janitors." I explained, hoping to ease some of the stress she had. I didn't blame her for getting upset, but it didn't make this conversation easy.

"How can you be sure? You can't possibly assume that," my mom countered, her voice becoming weaker and weaker.

"I know this isn't a good situation, but you're going to have to trust me. I've always stayed true to my word; why can't you trust me now?" I asked, hoping to end the conversation quickly. I didn't want to spend my last couple of days at home fighting. "You'll just have to get used to cooking only for Benry for a year," I joked, hoping to lighten up the mood.

"You know that your brother hates my cooking." My mom laughed, a smile finally creeping onto her face.

"Well he will have to learn to deal with it." I laughed again. "Speaking of your cooking, when's dinner, I'm starting to get hungry." I asked, my stomach rumbling in agreement.

"Well, since you are going away, I guess I should make your favorites. How about some roast beef? And we can have some burgers tomorrow." She suggested, wiping the tears from her face.

"Sounds great."

It has been two months since I've come to Vietnam, and it didn't take long to realize that this wasn't going to be easy.

"Hey Jeff. You ready to head out?" My new friend asked. Troy was a funny guy. He always had a goofy grin, always cracking jokes. That's important for morale. He could be serious at times too, though. Troy was practically perfect for this hell hole.

"Uh, yea. Just writing a letter home. Never know if you will be able to write again." I said, putting the letter in the envelope.

"Well, that's morbid. If you think like that than you will probably die. You just got to relax." Troy explained, using his hands to make overexerted movements.

"How can you relax in this kind of environment? With all the death?" I asked him, sticking the letter in my web gear. *Just in case.*

"If you're going to die, being stressed out about it won't change anything. Also, a friend told me bullets are afraid of courage. If you're not afraid of them, then they will miss. It's probably why they can't hit me, I'm too brave for that." He smiled and stood there triumphantly, as if he had just won something.

"Yea you're too a lot of things." I said, getting a chuckle from Troy. *Just be brave, can that really work?* Troy just stood there, smiling at me. *Damn he is goofy.*

"Well, let's get over there before we get yelled at. You know how pissed Brett can get." He reminded me, motioning for me to follow him.

"Yea you're right, no reason to get on that's jerk's bad side." I sighed, following him out to where the rest of the crew was. *Well, time to be brave.*

"Is that everyone? Alright. Time to get out there," he yelled as he led us out of the camp.

We walked for what felt like hours, and to make things worse we were walking without a single metal detector. We were just waiting for someone to die. "Are we almost to the village yet?" I grumbled, frustrated and bored.

"What, you bored? I can tell you that the village probably won't be entertaining. Even if we find some V.C, they will just be killed." Troy explained, waiving his gun around like an idiot.

"Shut up Troy!" Someone behind me yelled. "Stop taking this so lightly; we lost Jud last time we visited that village. The damn locals won't tell us were the V.C plant mines. If it were up to me, I would just torch the place and kill them for treason." The private behind me divulged, hate dripping from his words.

"Jack, did you just suggest we massacre them? They're just scared. You just can't kill people." I shot back. *I can't believe I'm forced to work with these sociopaths. He is no better than the VC.*

"Yea, well I'm pretty sure that Jud was scared when he found himself with no legs. How about his screams for help, or his pleas to God for mercy! How many people are you willing to let die before you see I'm right!" he screamed back. His face was bright red in anger.

"Hey! Lock it up back there. We're approaching the village!" Brett ordered from the front, an annoyed look on his face. "Look, we go in there. See if we find anything suspicious, and then we leave. Got it?" he asked in a demeaning tone.

"Got it" we all said in unison. No one was stupid enough to disobey Brett. He was almost as scary as the Viet Cong. Almost. We all split up into pairs, me and Troy went together as always.

"Who knows, maybe we might find a huge weapons cache hidden. That would for sure put a dent in their army," Troy fantasized, almost dancing into the village. 'I say we check the huts in the back, they usually don't hide that stuff at the front." He suggested, breaking into a light jog as we passed the wooden and straw buildings.

"Hey, wait for me!" I called out, following him down the dirt road. You could catch glimpses of the pure disgust that the villagers wore, not even trying to hide it. They just stood there staring at us. If they just told us where the VC hid their weapons and mines, then we wouldn't have to be here. It's their fault were here at all.

"Hey, look at this man." I heard Troy yell out. I stepped to his right and found myself staring at a white bunny. It kind of looked like the bunny mascot for the battery brand, with the toy drum it held. It was a pristine white, as if it had never been touched before. "Hey, you think the villagers will get mad if I take this?" he asked, examining the toy.

"Dude, the thing is like 3 feet tall! Do you really want to carry that all the way back?" I asked, questioning his logic. "Why is it even on the outskirts of this place, you would think it would be inside?" I thought out loud, still staring at the bunny.

"Who cares, I'll gift it to Brett. I can't wait to see his reaction." He chuckled, bending down to pick it up.

BOOM

I was quickly knocked to the ground, as I felt rain fall on top of me. "Hello?" I tried to yell out, but found I couldn't even hear myself through the constant ringing in my ears. Through a dazed look, I was able to see a bunch of people in green run up to me.

"Hey, hey Jeff. Can you hear me?" I faintly heard one of them yell. He started dragging me to the side as many other soldiers ran past me, to where a gaping hole was.

"Troy" I muttered, looking around for him.

"Troy? I don't see him, where is he?" The soldier who I identified as a medic asked. Another man walked over and showed us a bloody helmet.

"Oh shit, is that all that's left of him?" The medic asked. *Wait, him? No. That can't be.*

"From the looks of it." The other man sighed, dropping down on the ground.

"No." I groaned, feeling myself become dizzy. My hearing became fussy, my vision more blurred. *Troy can't be dead, he was the brave one.*

"So, you ready to get back to the states?" A man sitting next to me asked.

"Yea, I don't think I will ever forget what happened there though." I sighed, looking down at a silver tag. *Did I really deserve to live? Better people than me died. Why?*

"Who's that?" The man beside me asked, pointing towards the tag I held in my hand.

"His name was Troy. He was a goofy guy, but a good friend. At least, as good as a friend as you could have in country." I divulged, a tear forming in my eyes.

"You were infantry I'm guessing, right?" he asked with a concerned tone. His question almost made me laugh.

"Yea, who wasn't? They weren't drafting pep-talkers." I responded, a hint of anger in my voice.

"Yea, I guess it was kind of a stupid question." The guy apologized, rubbing his neck. "I don't think I got your name; I'm Grant." He introduced himself, reaching his hand out towards me.

"Jeff" I responded, shaking his hand. Grant talked for the rest of the flight, making it hard for me to shut him out. *I just need to make it back; I haven't survived yet,* I kept reminding myself. My heart was racing until the plane had landed on the runway.

"Well, it was nice meeting you." Grant said, a smile on his face. He got up and rushed off the plane, pushing two people aside to get off first.

"Well, he was annoying." I muttered out loud, gaining a laugh from someone behind me. I slowly stepped to the side, grabbing my duffel on the way out. I was blinded to the bright light, and as my eyes adjusted I could see a group of people, my brother Benry one of them. "Benry!" I called out, rushing towards him. He still wore those circle glasses, and that damn turtleneck. *Damn, he was a nerd.*

"Oh hey, you know that your plane was seven minutes late?" he asked, looking up from his watch.

"Shut up and come here." I laughed, putting him into a light choke hold. Tears formed in my eyes as I realized. *I made it.*

"Hey, don't be so rough," Benry complained, trying to push me off. I let him go, but quickly embraced him again, tears streaming down my face.

"I made it! I… I made it!" I sobbed, burrowing my head in his shoulder. My brother just stood there flabbergasted. He awkwardly patted me on the back.

"Let's go home Jeff."

"Thank you, mom. Your cooking is as good as always," I complimented, putting my dish in the sink.

"You always say that," She chuckled, scraping the plates clean.

"Well that's because it's always true." I laughed, walking back to the clean table. "Hey, where do you think Benry is? He is usually back by now." I asked, curious about my brother's location.

"I don't know, maybe he is…" She was interrupted by the door opening. My brother slowly walked in, not looking either of us in the eyes.

"Hey, what's wrong? Cheer up man, it can't be that bad," I expressed, walking towards him. *What is wrong with him? I've never seen him like this.* He didn't respond, instead he dropped an envelope on the table. My eyes widened at what I saw. *It was the same envelope that I had gotten two years ago.*

"Oh my god!" I heard my mom sob, she quickly ran over and hugged Benry, who still didn't move.

"No, they can't. They can't do this," she yelled out."

"Damn it." I sighed, my eyes not leaving the letter. There was no chance that Benry could survive out there; he wasn't strong enough. *If Troy couldn't survive out there, then there was no chance that my brother could. He was a dead man walking.*

"Mom," Benry whispered. "I don't want to die; please I don't want to die." My brother broke out, crying with my mom. *That's when it clicked. Only one of us could be forced on the battlefield. Had I never left, then he wouldn't had gotten that letter. I could survive better than him. I survived once. I could survive again.*

"Mom." I said, interrupting her moment. She looked over to me, confusion and anger painted on her face. "I'm going to talk to a recruiter, see what I have to do to enlist." I told her, a definitive tone fitting my voice.

"What do you mean, you're leaving too?" she asked, the anger leaving, just being replaced with more confusion.

"I can substitute for Benry, so he won't have to go. I can survive; hell I might even be able to make officer. That would mean I wouldn't be in the field as much." I explained to her. *It's the only way.*

"But you have been home for less than a year! You can't possibly go back!" she yelled.

"I can survive mom, I did once before. Do you really want to make Benry go?" I shot back, pointing to my sniffling brother. "I already made up my mind. I'm going to go back." My mom stood their silently, and gave me a subtle nod. *Damn, where is the nearest recruiter.*

It had been 5 months since I came back to this country, and it was the same hell as when I left it. I had been promoted to a squad leader, but that didn't mean less combat. "Alright, listen up. Today we are going to storm hill 937. We will have mortar and artillery fire soften them up; then we will storm the hill. Get ready to move out!" I ordered. I had a bad feeling in my gut.

"Sir, are you alright? Sir!" I heard a muffled voice call out. *Is this hell?* I wondered, feeling immense pain in my head. My vision started to clear, and I saw Sam running to my side. "Sir, what do we do?" he asked, noticing my lack of responsiveness. I slowly got up, reaching for my rifle.

"I thought I was dead," I muttered, looking at the tree that was now split even more. *The bullet hit the tree? I'm alive?* I questioned, looking at my hands.

"Sir, we've lost a lot of people. What do we do?" Sam questioned me again, intense fear in his face. I scanned the jungle around me, and saw several soldiers pinned down. *That bullet was inches from killing me, yet I'm alive. God must still want me to do something. To take this hill?* I thought, grabbing my rifle and checking the magazine. *It's now or never.*

"Damn It!" I screamed, jumping over my cover, and running further up the hill. *I would take out as many as possible, that I was sure of.* I jumped into a makeshift trench, surprising to N.V.A. I pulled the trigger, and they both fell to the ground, only one letting out a cry.

"GI!" I heard one of them scream. I jumped out of the trench, and ran further up the hill. The cackling sounds of bullets ricocheting could be heard, some much louder than others. *Come on, let's go!* I saw another one, frantically trying to reload his rifle. I didn't wait, shooting him twice in the chest. I could see what I thought was the top, then a loud thud. I looked to my side to see at least 4 of them, all aiming at me.

"Shit" I mumbled, before a third gunshot surprised us both. I looked back to see Sam right behind me. Not just Sam, but at least 5 others. *They followed me?* The N.V.A were gunned down, yelping for what I could imagine was help.

"For America!" I heard someone around me scream. A smile crept over my face. *We could do this.* Me and my men ran up the hill dodging in an out of the fallen trees and makeshift bunkers. The Vietnamese weren't trying to win anymore, many fleeing further up the hill.

"The top! We're almost there." I bellowed to my men. We approached the top, and the long-range battle quickly became a close-range one. One of them pounced me, trying to stab me with a knife. I fought to hold up his hand, before knocking him over. This is for Troy! I thought as I unhooked my helmet and knocked the knife out of his hands. I jumped on top of him and started to hit him with the helmet. First once, then twice. I wasn't going to risk it, I kept hitting him and hitting him. Blood spurted over my face, but I didn't stop, soon his face was unrecognizable, and I threw my helmet to the side, falling over next to him.

"Did you find all the Vietnamese weapons?" I asked some privates, just sitting on the ground, all of them wearing grim faces. One of them pointed to a tree with a wooden sign stuck to it with a bloody bayonet.

Hamburger hill
My ears seemed to open, as the screams of the wounded filled my ears. "Oh my god." I gasped, looking at my bloody hands. I looked at the dead troops that had been dragged to the top. Some missing arms, some legs. And the expressions of those that still had heads, *Pure terror*. I fell to the ground, trying to wipe the blood from my hands, but no matter how much I tried, it wouldn't come off. *Why won't it come off? What is this? What did we do?* My thoughts flashed back to my last tour, and I pulled the tag that had been in my pocket. "Was it worth it, was all this really worth it?"

"That's up to the body count." One of the silent privates spoke out. "We just took on a human meat grinder. You should be happy you survived," the private suggested.

"Surviving isn't enough," I mumbled, looking up to the sky. *I should have died. Why did you not kill me God?*

"As if the private could read my thoughts, he stated, "They die, so we can go home."

"And do we deserve to go home, have we earned that right?" I asked, emphasizing the we.

"Well, sir." another private said, nervously rubbing his neck behind me.

"You can stop using that sir shit with me. Just tell me, do we deserve to survive?" I asked, my voice becoming frantic and wild.

"Of course, we do," he responded, using a more sure tone.

I stood there, the screams of the dead still filling my ears. "Why?" I asked.

He stood there, pondering my question, finally he looked back at me. "I guess it is just God's will. It's all part of his master plan," he suggested with a defeated shrug.

"You believe in God, how? Why is God doing this?" I asked, a hint of envy in my voice. Not because of his answer, but because he could still believe in God. He hadn't lost the hope I and so many others lost long ago.

"I don't know, I'm not a prophet. I just know that I am alive, and that must be a reason," he explained, rubbing his neck again. *Could I blame him, I was basically interrogating the poor private?*

"Alright, get back to work." I ordered, walking away, trying to get away from the bodies that were getting piled up. I just need to survive.

"You wanted to speak with me, sir?" I asked as I entered the green tent. He sat there, in his leather chair. He had a pretty bored look on his face, examining something on his desk. He quickly looked up, and put on a fake smile.

"Welcome Jeff, look. We reviewed the work you did on hill 937, and to say we were impressed wouldn't be the half of it. We just wanted you to know that we were impressed. Good work, soldier." He finished, standing up to salute me. I saluted back, and he slumped back into his chair. I started to walk away, but stopped.

"Sir," I started, turning to face my CO. "The battle of hamburger hill, will it be considered a win?" I asked, my voice becoming shaky as I choked on the words.

"Hamburger hill? You mean hill 937; of course we will, it was an overwhelming success," he responded, while writing something down.

"Sir, what is wrong with you? How can you consider that a win? We couldn't even tell some of the bodies apa- "

"That's enough, you better hold your tongue." He shook his head and looked down at his desk, took a deep breath, and looked back up. "Look Sergeant . . ."

I pulled on the stripes on my sleeve. "I was squad leader, but I'm still a corporal."

"You've been promoted. And I know what you are thinking. Why? Why, are we doing this? Why are there so many dead? Why am I still alive? What's the point? Everyone that has seen combat asks these questions. I don't have an answer, but I don't need one. As a soldier we obey orders, the decisions are above our pay grade."

"Maybe that is the point, Sir. The decision to kill someone shouldn't be above anyone's pay grade."

He just stared at me. "Dismissed." He motioned me to leave. I didn't even salute him, I just left, my fist in balls.

TIME

Sara Kates and Sam Horton

We are the Creators,

We are the Destroyers,

We are Order,

We are Chaos,

And as the Sun began to rise,

On that very day,

The dawn of time…

The Genesis…

There would be Balance,

Day by day,

Hour by hour,

They do what they can,

They don't do enough

And they set the pendulum in motion,

They work for righteousness,

They allow darkness to consume,

They are naïve,

They are arrogant,

They cannot be held accountable,

They must be punished,

For the destruction of Nature,

They do not know,

It is in their blood,

They are more than monsters,

No more than savages,

They must be saved,

They must be destroyed,

There must be Balance,

Something must be done,

Now

Nature

Geethika Kataru

The fields of grass surround me
The waves of the ocean say hello
The trees grow tall and proud around me
The flurry of winter snow falls on my nose

The beauty of nature reminds me
That humans get so wrapped up in hate
We forget the love that forged us
Created us from stardust
And kissed our cheeks

The fierceness of nature reminds me
That humans forget where they came from
We must remember that the force of love
Heals our hearts
    And wipes our violence away

Midnight's Flower

Erica Catanzarite

The moon in the sky
is hidden from sight
cloaked in
the thickening clouds.

The shadows cast
by the dying flowers
resembles dead bodies,
mangled by war.

And as the wind picks up
the night's silence
is only interrupted
by the hissing of dead grass.

The dark night
makes my heart beat in fear

Yet something makes me stop.

A single flower
blooms in the field
illuminated by a sliver of moon.

And my remaining fear
dissipates like fog
as I stare

at that single,

glowing

flower.

Solace

Sammy Horton

It was abnormally quiet on that day,
and nobody believed it would be that way
when expectation demanded celebration
one that would rattle the whole nation.

There was none.

Instead of cheering, whooping, laughing, and crying,
all that could be heard was the tranquil sighing,
the sound of a light snoring trailed from a boy,
as he slept in his bed in a peaceful joy.

To him, the world was quiet and still,
as moonlight filtered through his window sill,
no wars, no quarrels, no fight of any kind,
could be brought to the forefront of the mind.

And though some did not see this magnificent sight,
in their own ways, they appreciated the most silent of nights.

Utopia

Lorelai Veedvick

A day without wives weeping
over husbands, and mothers
over sons.
A day without children being
beaten by parents.

A day where the only tears
are happy ones.

Where children aren't gunned
down in schools.
Where people aren't killed
simply for
who they are
who they love
what skin color they have
what religion they are.

A day without violence

Tomorrow

Kenneth Austin

A day where no bullets
are fired

When people drop their
rifles

Where men can leave the
trenches

And embrace the men
they once saw as enemies

Forgetting the horrors
they once witnessed

To return home to their
friends and family

To a world without violence

Universal Love Song

Jennifer Sloan

Imagine entire solar systems displayed all around you
and you can see every single star in the universe.
There's dwarf planets and nebulas
and every single star is different.
Some are blue and some a dazzling white.
And even the black holes, terrifying at first,
have an unequaled sense of awe to them.
The sun in this solar system is shining on you,
and the moon is smiling at her.
Now imagine waking in a flower field,
with millions of flowers around you.
Daffodils, and Chamomiles, and Daisy's.
Greens and yellows and pinks.
And some might be missing a petal
But they're still gorgeous.

If everything in the universe is different but still beautiful,
shouldn't we be?

The stars and the nebulas are all different sizes and colors
but still provoke a sense of wonder.
The flowers are all unique and flawed but are still praised
for their beauty.
Take a lesson from the Earth,
treat everyone with the same wonder you received
from the stars.
the same gentleness you gave the flowers,

and maybe then, we could have
a world without violence.

Acceptance

To rise beyond the hate and violence of this world we must begin to accept each other for who we really are. Obviously the authors of the following pieces do not wish to live in a society where we are all the same perfect copies of some abstract ideal. They realize that the most glorious thing about human beings is what is unique about each of us. When we all embrace the diversity and uniqueness of humanity, the whole becomes better than a life divided.

Porcelain

Becca Jaeger

We're all held in potter's hands.
We've all been molded
into beautiful works of art.
We're all made of clay.
We're all filled with hope.
Joy fills us up to the brim,
overflowing from our souls.
We've all got cracks and chips.
But when we're put side by side,
we're a molded work of art,
a porcelain America.

WOMAN

Maddie Lower

How do you see me?
Short?
Weak?
Less than you?

I see myself as me
I'm not here to be labeled
I'm not here for you
I'm here to change the world

I'm a person, not a doll
I can choose what I wear
How I do my hair
Who I am

I choose to be strong
I choose to be smart
I choose to be the revolution
FOR I AM: WOMAN.

Inheritance

Madi Bishop

I am a collection of my attributes
I am all of myself
I am a sum of ancestral traits
I am myself and no one else
I am my curly brown hair
that catches the golden sun
I am my thoughtful eyes
full of wonder and depth
I am a brain, a great mind
valued for its maturity and wit
I am my Father's angels
a face 'masculine and geometric'
I am my mother's illnesses
and her jittery 'anxious tic'
I am my aunt's womanly figure
with hips and thighs that match
I am my uncle's knack for language

I am my grandfather's liberal ways
all of his opinions and views
I am my grandmother's memory fade
her trouble with names and dates
I am my grandma's poised exterior
and inner chaos to which I can relate
I am my papa's motor head
situated between two shoulders of steel
I am his caring soul
and his emphatic feel
I am his good spirits
I am his good intentions
I am all of them, with a twist
all of their facets and qualities.

Us

Ray Vanover

We have celebrations
We have parades
We have riots
And marches

We celebrate winning a war
But protest guns
We groan when we see two men kissing
But egg them on when they're fighting
We march for recognition
But rally against people

When will enough be enough
When will we celebrate our individuality
When will we learn to compromise
It's not all about us
as one person
But us as a whole.

On This Day

Becca Jaeger

*The light dancing
of people's feet
mingling with the bouncing
notes of music
Hand in hand
enjoying each other's unique
style
The mixture of people
the same notes
in different sequences
The same joy
filling different hearts
on this day
full of faith, grace, and peace*

Deafness

Natalia Camacho

Silence
That's all I can hear,
Not a single sound.
I see people open their mouths
And not a single sound comes out.
They seem unaffected by it.
Everywhere, sounds are made,
But I cannot hear it.
Cannot hear the birds,
Cannot hear the trains go by,
Cannot hear the family speak.
How I wonder what sounds are.

Then a switch turned on,
Sounds have dropped on me like a bomb.
All different sounds combined together.
The sounds of people and so much more.
I cannot take it anymore.
A switch turned off,
Sounds disappeared from my world.
Not a single thing disturbed,
Sometimes silence is golden.

Soft Touches

Annalise Imperato

I am not quirky
I am not strange
I am autistic
we're misunderstood.
No one makes an effort to make things easier
They call our self-regulations weird and make us stop
So we sit there until we can't take it
It's too much
The world is closing in
Something touches you and you smack it away
Then people are angry.
But what else are you supposed to do when you hate
Those soft touches?
When you feel unsafe and unsure

We are portrayed as rude
Male
White
Young
Math-loving
 and cold
instead of
creative
smart
diverse
friendly
and empathetic.

They say we feel nothing but many of us feel too much
We feel when others are happy
when they are confused
when they talk about us as if we aren't in the room
and it hurts.
But no one cares about the "special kid".

Spoons

Ray Vanover

5:30 am

I have 6 spoons. I get up I eat and then brush my teeth. I never brush my teeth before I eat. That tastes weird and makes my tongue feel like it's covered in this icky gunk kind of like mucus but worse.

6:00 am

I take a shower ten minutes no longer, water is itchy, feels like sweat then I feel dirty all over again.

7:00 am

Fridays are always *Big Bang Theory* any other day is some crime show of my choice. Mrs. Paige says I need to change one thing in my routine a week. I found a way to change it without changing it. It's Friday, *Big Bang Theory* isn't recorded. Today's gonna be a bad day.

8:00 am

I need my shoes. Slip-ons are less trouble but they rub against my ankles. I don't like it, all I can hear is rubbing, but when I get home I can take them off easy. I'll wear slip-ons.

8:20 am

I need to walk to my friend's house or we're gonna be late. School starts at 9:15 always early never late if you're late you can't go.

9:15 am

4 spoons. I have 4 I saw my girlfriend she seemed mad but she's not a morning person that's on my list of things she told me. It's loud, I sit next to a boy who's always eating in 1st period his food smells bad I always try to tell him he thinks I'm joking.

9:50 am

I get to leave early I'll walk to 2nd before the hallways get too loud.

10:00 am

I hate it in here, it always smells like Goodwill. I don't like that smell.

4:30 pm

It's been an okay day.

5:30 pm

My mom told me my cousins are coming. I can't miss school. I want to but I can't, school is my routine and not keeping that routine would not be okay. I don't know my cousins, it's new, new is bad.

7:30 am

They're coming today. Mom said it's okay. It's not okay.

8:30 am

They're here, their mom has an odd shape. She looks friendly. They're young. Maybe this will be nice.

9:00 am

I was wrong, they're touching my stuff. I don't remember where everything was and now everything's in a new place. It'll never be in the same place again.

9:15 am

They touched my stuff now they're touching me, they're hands are gritty and they smell like baby formula.

9:30 am

My mom told them to calm down. It's not working. I had 7 spoons this takes 8 spoons but I can make it.

9:45 am

They like sharks so I showed them my shark teeth, they liked my shark teeth. We have something to talk about.

11:45 am

It's lunch time. Mom made something different for lunch. I always eat hot pockets for lunch she made soup. They're messy eaters like sharks. They're a lot like sharks actually.

1:00 pm

This isn't so bad now that they're sharks but I'm ready for them to leave.

1:30 pm

They're gone. I'm kinda lonely now.

Editor's note:

For some individuals on the autistic spectrum, every action of daily life requires a certain amount of energy. In this story it was represented as *spoons* in the main character's mind. Daily situations require less or more spoons, resulting in how well they are able to deal with it. For instance, the little cousins created a situation causing more stress, which required eight spoons. The main character felt they only had seven spoons, thus creating a specific social situation, which was difficult. If you think about it, we all have a certain amount of *spoons* with us. Day in and day out, we are required to use our spoons to make it through every aspect of life, the countless situations we may face. While we cannot say for sure, we suspect that there are people, on and off the spectrum, who are more keenly aware of this than the rest of us. And perhaps, we have something to learn from them about coping.

Is

Katie Kelsey

Henry and Fallon.
Two lovers: high school sweethearts.
Nobody denied them.
No one dared to.
What is this?
This is Love.

Jessica and Tyler.
Married only after a year.
The biggest mistake of his life.
Crying, on the floor with bruises littering his body.
What is this?
This is not Love.

James and Philip.
Friends since 3rd grade.
But, in sophomore year, something changed.
More than friends, they claimed.
What is this?
This is Love.

Kyle and Mark.
Junior year of high school, they begun.
"More than friends!" Kyle cried.
"I love you!" Kyle cried. Mark cringed.
What is this?
This is not Love.

Rose and Sarah
Met at a college frat party.
Their eyes met and their cheeks flushed.
They talked for hours, hearts in their eyes.
What is this?
This is Love.

Mariah and Jeff.
Met in a not-so-hot spot of a bar.
Jeff dropped a pill into her drink,
Desperate for her to be his.
What is this?
This is not Love.

Jackson and Leo.
Leo: born into the wrong family.
But, thankfully, rose above it all.
Leo's situation didn't matter to Jackson.
What is this?
This is Love.

Nicole and Izzy.
Both dating and head-over-heels.
Izzy sees someone new and falls,
Falls into another's arms, while still in Nicole's.
What is this?
This is not Love.

Love is two or more people,
Caring for,
Waiting for,
Bettering
Each other.

Love is Love.

Heartfelt

Nia Howard

Love is a powerful thing
It can melt the coldest of hearts
It can heal the largest of wounds.

Love is known here
It lives in my heart,
the home that follows me everywhere.

Love grows here,
where blood flows red
and flowers bloom

Love lives here
where kindness is warmth
and this heart beats

It travels through every vein
and settles in every bone

Love grows here, here in my home.

Diverse

Erin Vogel

Fresh apples in a basket,
All clean: red, green and yellow.
Eaten by children whose skin differ in hues.
The adults crowd together in conversation
With drinks and jokes, laughter and smiles.
Spoken in languages from around the world.

The adults don't always agree,
The children don't always play fair.
But they do not fight, scream and yell and cry.
They find a solution for their differences.
And though their interests aren't alike,
They leave their differences behind.

Awareness

And yet there are some things we should not accept. The mantra "but things have always been this way" has been spoken too many times in our history and has impeded man's progress toward creating a better world. Humans fear change, and it is okay to acknowledge that fear. But as the following authors point out, we cannot grow and evolve to something greater without moving beyond that fear. Our awareness is essential and our voices must not be silent.

Common Sense

by
Sam Binard

Pressed against a parchment sheet

the pen

cries out against injustice..

What kind of world

allows the hate to prosper?

What kind of people

allow this to transpire?

Crying out against violence

pressed against a parchment sheet

the flow of a quill continues on.

The Nature of Revolutions

Tyler Danson

I hear the trumpets blow
But they do not sound the same
Instead of pride, there's envy
Instead of sorrow, there's shame

I hear the anthems sung
But the notes seem all dreary
And foreign to the ears
But not the least too teary

The parade marches on
Each soldier, rank and file
Where not the bravest men
Would care to stay awhile

In your revolution
Did reveling take the wheel?
Or envy give way to lust
To make the robbed want to steal?

In your quest for truth
How many lies did you tell?
On the crusade for logic
What virtue did you sell?

A nation lies in ruins
A government overthrown
Their tyranny defeated
To replace it with your own

You see there's little difference
Between the predator and their prey
For once its laws are broken
Nature must obey

Even though you've destroyed it all
I'll not let passion burn to hate
a senseless waste of honor
For one with a sealed fate

Returning from my funeral
You may count it as a win
and I'll be glad to see you
When the trumpets blow again

No News is Still News

Malea Jones

I'd rather not watch the news today;
I already know what they're going to say
Too much to report, no new words to convey
'cause
"things have always been this way."
I wonder why.

I'd rather not watch the news tonight,
'cause shooting stars, shining bright
don't cease the shooting that fill me
and my brother with fright.
'cause
to be a child with skin that isn't white
is to be labeled before you can even understand
"Why do cashiers only watch me so closely?"
I no longer have to wonder why.

I'd rather not watch the news this week.
'cause even if it's good (for once) I won't speak
for each spark of hope reminds me that
my father won't agree
'cause
even though there's thousands of new rights
for ten million people just like me, just like everyone,
"suicide is the second leading cause of death
Among LGBT+ teens and young adults, behind murder."
Does no one wonder why?

I'd rather not watch the news again
with its plastic colors and plastic men
and women, too, but who remembers them?
How is my friend supposed to marry rich

when her and her wife will be making
"only 78 percent of a man's dollar"?
Representation?
"Women aren't watching this!"
I wonder, why not?

I'd rather not watch the news, oh please!
we all know that we're going to see
Some "nice guy" that couldn't let some girl be
(if he plays sports, throws a ball, he'll go free).
and the TV will remind us
How much promise he had
Ignoring the life he left in shambles
"one in four women and one in four men will
be sexually assaulted in their lifetime" studies show
Why aren't they asking why?

I'd rather not watch the news at all
So please turn off the box on the wall
Cause in a world so large I've never felt so small
We do our best
To live, to breathe, to fight
Only to see the same crushing truths each night
"Things have always been this way!"
Why haven't we been asking why?

My Dream

Ainsley Dysart

I am thirteen
I have a dream
But I have games and sports
that I should be playing
My dream can wait

I am sixteen
I have a dream
But I have teachers and friends
that I should be impressing
My dream can wait

I am eighteen
I have a dream
But I have a job
that I should be doing
My dream can wait

I am twenty-three
I have a dream
But I am getting married
My dream can wait

I am thirty-three
I have a dream
But I have kids
that I must be chasing
My dream can wait

I am forty-three
I have a dream
But my kids are graduating
My dream can wait

I am fifty-three

I have a dream
But I have retirement
that I have to be planning
My dream can wait

I am sixty-three
I have a dream
But I have cancer
that I have to be fighting
My dream can wait

I am seventy-three
I have dream
But the lights are fading
My dream can't come true

Editor's Note:

Everyone has dreams, and many don't come true.
But don't wait for your dreams, you must pursue:
the only chance your dream has, is you.

All American Dream

Victoria Rachal

Dreamers,
We're just a bunch of Dreamers,
Looking for a chance to make a change
for ourselves,
for our families,
for our loved ones.

Some are born into the American Dream,
the rest of us have to fight.

We fight to prove
to ourselves,
to our families,
and to those who think we can't,
that we will persevere

Some of you fly like the eagle,
gracefully taking in your freedoms,
scouting your victims with ease,
and attacking without remorse.

Attacking us,
the Dreamers,
filling us with doubt,
tearing families apart...

They are the watchers,
Watching as our countries go to ruins,
Watching as our families fill with grief,

Watching and doing nothing.

They deny access to safety
as we pound on the door
attempting to escape our personal hell
But they are blinded by their version
of the American Dream.

The American Dream to you:
it sounds like laughter,
the roar of an engine,
the quiet chirps of a bird,
all things of beauty and grace...

We only wish that it sounded
the same for all.

Thumper

Becca Jaeger

6/16/2007

Dear diary, Cici, my best friend, got a bunny!!!!!!!!!!!!!!!!!!!! She named him Donald, continuing her family's tradition of naming their pets after Disney characters. She let me come over to her house today to see him. She said they're making him a show bunny. They have several show bunnies, but this one is only Cici's. I can't wait to go back tomorrow and play with her bunny more, he's so cute!!!!!!!

8/20/2007

Dear diary, we started school today. I have a feeling first grade is going to be the best year ever!!!! Everybody loves Cici! They all want to go over to her house to see Donald! My best friend is becoming popular! That means I can become popular, too! My older sister, Hannah, tells me being popular is very important, and very impressive. I don't know what impressive means, but it sounds good.

9/13/2007

Dear diary, today Cici betrayed me, as Hannah would say. Last night, Katie went over to Cici's house to play with Donald. And I wasn't invited. And now, Katie is calling herself Cici's best friend! That's supposed to be me! Katie claims she knows EVERYTHING about Cici's bunny, but she only spent one day with Donald! I doubt she even saw him jump. Cici says bunnies jump when they get happy. I've seen him do it. It's cute. Katie is dumb. She's fat and dumb and only knows two words, so and cute.

11/17/2007

Dear diary, I am officially mad at Cici forever. She is no longer my best friend. Katie still insists on being Cici's best friend, and now she can be. Cici's birthday party was today. She turned eight. She had it at her house so everyone could see her stupid bunny. And she told me she could make me popular at her party. But she didn't. She forgot I was there! She was having so much fun with all her popular friends while I sat alone by her stupid bunny's cage. I thought he spoke to me. I told him I refused to call him Donald anymore. He's a stupid bunny, not a real pet. He doesn't fetch, and I would never tell a bunny my secret; they have gross teeth. Cici just shows him off, she doesn't keep him as a real pet to make herself happy. I said all of that to him when I sat alone by his pen. But he just jumped around. Then I realized, as he was jumping, he was speaking to me. His mouth wasn't moving; I know bunnies can't actually talk, but I heard his words in my mind. I couldn't understand what he was saying, because it was all adult language, but I got one thing. He told me that he did make Cici happy, because he made her popular. I guess that's true. The only thing that made Cici popular was her bunny, not herself.

11/18/2007

Dear diary, I dreamt about a bunny last night. Not Cici's stupid bunny, but a different bunny. His teeth weren't as gross and he didn't speak to me with words I couldn't understand. He told me that I could become popular if I did what he said. He told me Cici is going to ask me to watch her stupid bunny while she visits her Grandma, and if I have the stupid bunny, everybody will want to come over to my house to play with him. That's how I can become popular. I don't know when Cici is going to visit her Grandma, because we have school. But I wish the dream came true.

11/20/2007

Dear diary, the dream came true. Cici said she has to visit her Grandma because her Grandma needs help or something, and she asked me to watch her stupid bunny! She said that her mom doesn't trust Katie, so ha for Katie! She's dumb anyways, the bunny probably wouldn't last a day if she was watching him.

11/23/2007

Dear diary, Cici is gone, and everybody wants to come over to my house tomorrow to see her stupid bunny. Katie keeps saying we should leave Cici's bunny alone, since he is a show bunny and needs his beauty sleep. But I said it's okay, and now everybody loves me! So ha, Katie!

11/24/2007

Dear diary, today was a great day! A lot of people came over to see the bunny. He hasn't said a single word to me since her party; I'm pretty sure I imagined all of that. But there was another bunny in his pen today. It was the bunny from my dream. Cici's bunny didn't seem to notice it, and neither did my friends. He just sat there and did nothing. But my friends loved seeing Cici's stupid bunny and playing around with him. They all think I'm super awesome for watching Cici's pet for her. Hopefully I won't need the stupid bunny for them to want to come over again! I had a lot of fun today.

136

12/3/2007

Dear diary, Cici and I are best friends again. Cici finally realized how dumb Katie is and told her they can't be friends anymore. Cici says I did a great job watching Donald, and everybody thought that was awesome! They all want us to play together on Saturday!

12/25/2007

Dear diary, Christmas was fun! I got a lot of stuff. That bunny I keep seeing watched me as I opened every present. He told me I could have gotten better presents, but nobody else heard him.

1/1/2008

Dear diary, last night, I ate a lot of ice cream. The bunny told me I should take all that I wanted. Kyle called me greedy, but I don't know what that means. But now I feel sick.

5/15/2008

Dear diary, school is out! We are going to be second graders next year!! I am so excited! This summer is going to be the best! Cici and I have been invited to several pool parties, and Cici says I can go with her to a bunny show sometime this summer! I can't wait!

6/19/2008

Dear diary, I decided to name the bunny I keep seeing. I think Donald is a stupid name for a bunny, and I told Cici that when she got him. But she refused to name him Thumper, even though that's still a Disney character. So, I decided to name my bunny Thumper. He's a proper pet, because I don't show him off to people, and he makes me happy. I can tell him all of my secrets, even the ones I write in here, because nobody can ever take secrets out of him, because he can't talk. Even though he talks to me, I know nobody else can see him.

8/18/2008

Dear diary, second grade started today! I am still popular. Hannah said I had to be careful, because sometimes you come back from summer break and your popularity is gone. But mine is not, and neither is Cici's. Katie got held back. She was dumb anyways.

10/23/2011

Dear diary, I found this as I was cleaning my room today. I completely forgot about it. I've missed several years. But I'm in fifth grade now, and it's a lot of fun! My older sister says I should be getting into boys, now. I think I kind of like Trevor. He's funny. But Cici likes him, too. She told me she likes him. Thumper says I should tell Trevor that I like him. I think I will.

10/28/2011

Dear diary, I told Trevor that I like him. He told me he likes me, too. He wants to go trick-or-treating with me on Halloween. The problem is, I always go with Cici. He said I could invite her, but I don't want to that, because she'll be angry with me if she finds out that Trevor likes me, and if she finds out that I told him I like him. Thumper says I should just tell Cici I can't go trick-or-treating at all this year.

11/1/2011

Dear diary, Cici found out about Trevor and me. Trick-or-treating with him was a lot of fun, but Thumper kept following us around, even though I wanted him to go away. This morning, there were two bunnies in my room. I told the other one to go away, but it wouldn't. Thumper said she was his friend. Cici says we are no longer friends, but Thumper's bunny friend told me that I don't need Cici, because I have Trevor and Thumper and her. I've decided to name her Flower.

12/18/2011

Dear diary, last night, I told my parents about Trevor. Dad says I am too young to date, but Mom told him it was just a phase. I said it's not, and that I really like Trevor, and now I'm grounded. It's not fair. Hannah keeps laughing at me. Thumper and Flower tell me it's not fair for her to be able to like boys just because she's older. I tried saying that to Mom and Dad, but they just got angrier.

4/23/2012

Dear diary, Trevor and I have been dating in secret and last night we went to the Spring Fling. I ran into Cici there and we decided we were best friends again, since she's now dating Garret and doesn't like Trevor, anymore. But Trevor decided he doesn't like me, anymore. He told me he wants to date Cici, and asked me if I could set them up, since I was her friend. So Cici and I ditched both boys and had fun at the Spring Fling ourselves. The bunnies won't leave me alone and keep asking me to feed them. But they aren't really there... I'm not sure what I'm supposed to feed them.

9/22/2013

This is no longer a diary. Cici says diaries are uncool. We are in middle school now, and in order to be popular, you have to be cool. Thumper and Flower are telling me a lot of ways I can be cool. I'm starting to think it's not right, though, because it might hurt others' feelings. But Thumper and Flower told me it's okay. They said this is how I feed them. I'm not sure what that means, but if it'll get them to stop bugging me about feeding them... Middle school is hard. I have a lot of work and I have to stay up later to do it all. School also starts earlier than elementary school did, so I'm really tired all the time. So I guess I won't be writing in here as much, especially since it might not be cool.

08/13/2015

138

I stumbled across this again while I was rearranging my room before high school starts. I was dumb as a kid. I had a lot of petty fights with Cici, way more than were recorded here. She's still my best friend, and we're wiser, now. We don't fight over boys, anymore. We make them fight over us. Hannah says that's how it's supposed to be done. I'm not jealous of Cici's bunny… that she still has... Apparently, bunnies can last a long time when you take care of them. I thought they only lasted, like, four years, but Donald is eight, now.

My bunnies are still around, too. They're extremely hard to take care of, they demand a lot. They don't really eat anything. And they don't have a cage, no bedding, and there aren't any messes to clean up. But they still require a lot, for some reason. I started thinking frequently throughout middle school that I'm going mad. I mean, I'm seeing animals that aren't really there, and nobody else can see them… and they talk to me. Does that count as hearing voices in my head? People who hear voices in their head are mad… but the bunnies are my pets. They comfort me and help me. I still tell them all of my secrets, and they tell me things to do. I'm not so worried about being cool, anymore. Hannah says that popularity doesn't matter anymore, because once you get out of high school, nobody cares. I am worried about success, though. Everybody talks about high school as a big competition. I have to have the highest GPA, the most impressive test scores, great relationships with teachers, and impressive volunteer services in order to get into college and have a successful life. I want to be better than everyone else. The bunnies keep telling me exactly how I can do that. I've realized that every time I talk about wanting success over everyone else, the bunnies stop complaining about being fed. I kind of wish they would talk the way they did when I was little and thought they were speaking in "adult language." I could probably make sense of it, now. But there are so many of them, I can barely tell who's talking all at one time. There's still Thumper, and Flower, but there's also Bambi, Friend Owl (who I just call Owl), Ronno, and Faline, all characters from Bambi. They just seem to keep growing. I'm worried that it's going to get out of control, but they're just bunnies, they can be domesticated.

05/22/2019

I'm so bad at keeping up with this thing. I didn't lose it this time, but every time I tried to pick it up to write in it, I got distracted. I've been so busy, I've just forgotten about this. But I still have my bunnies. I've given up on naming them all, because they just keep multiplying. But they all seem to know my name, whispering "Jane! Jane!" every time they want something. There are too many bunnies telling me what to do, and demanding to be fed. Maybe I can just leave them all behind for college, and just take Thumper and Flower with me. Right now, all these bunnies are messing with my relationships. I had a boyfriend for awhile. Mark was great, and he said he loved me. Even Dad liked him. But after awhile, he said I was too wrapped up in success that I was trampling over others to get to it, and I didn't care about anyone else but myself. But that's not true! I decided he's just a jerk, but when I told Cici about it, she said she agreed with him!

Well, graduation was today. Now I can go off to my dream school, UCF, and become the greatest engineer there ever was, and not have to worry about Cici or Mark ever again. I can start new, with better friends. Thumper says I don't need any friends, because I have him and the rest of the bunnies. But I'm not so excited about that.

6/16/36

Today, I saw a bunny in the kitchen. I gave Wesley and Ben cake and Wesley ate his faster. I saw him staring at Ben while he savored his, and then I saw the bunny whispering in Wesley's ear. So I told him to go play outside and let Ben finish his ice cream in peace. Then I told the bunny to leave my sons alone. I know Josh would be proud.

All I Know

Supriya Pali

I am a dog. That I know.

That is what Man would call me. With a "here dog" and a rough swat, I was to obey his every command. I fetched things. I went places. I delivered messages. I greeted the boy across the street. It was my duty. And it was the same, every day.

Man changed over time. This I noticed. When I first met him, he was strong. He would run along by my side in the fields. He would drop down into the grass and laugh. A wide grin on his face, as the deep sound resonated through my heart. He would then look softly into my eyes, and I would perk up. Because I knew.

But now, Man does not step foot outside our shabby, wooden shelter. He sits in the rocking chair by the window with a new emptiness in his eyes. Sometimes he would look down at his hands, those marked with scars and creases. I would bring over the silver tin, as I was told. I would watch him pop out bullets and drop them down his throat. He would grimace, and I would whimper. But he would always look into my eyes and whisper the same thing: "hush dog." And I would, as I was told.

Man was gone a long time now. He often was. He would leave for what seemed like forever, only to come back more broken than before. During these times I stayed with "Old Woman." That is what man called her. He would leave me with her with a slam of the door and "mother" on his lips. Old Woman stayed past the fields by the river. Every day, we went down to the riverbank together. We would pick berries from the thick bushes and catch fish in the skittish waters. I would splash and paw the water as Old Woman watched, a tender smirk on her face. But sometimes, Old Woman would get dangerously close to the water and drop to her knees. She would raise her arms to the sky and chant words that I did not understand. That was when I would miss Man the most.

Today for the first time, I saw Old Woman cry. Someone had come to the door with a message. As soon as Old Woman had looked at it, tears began to fall down her face. I went by her side. Her frail hands sunk deep into my back. I could feel her weight upon my shoulders. After that, Old Woman was also gone for a while. She left me with food, water, and a touch on the head. I waited and watched by the window for her return. That too made me miss Man.

Old Woman finally came back. But with the same emptiness in her wrinkled eyes as Man had by the window. We went down to the river, but this time we crossed over on an unsteady bridge. Beyond the river was a meadow of pure, white flowers. But we went even further. We went through a light forest to barren land. The land was scattered with spaced out stones that stuck out of the ground.

I perked up; I could sense Man. He was summoning me. I ripped away from Old Woman's side to run to him. I reached the fresh stone where Man was. Old Woman followed me with new tears in her eyes. I could not understand, but I knew man was there. I lay down with my head between my paws by Man's place. I was prepared to wait forever.

Because I was dog. And that I knew.

Hope

With awareness comes hope; and while ethereal, hope is the tiny light in the darkness that cannot be extinguished. The quiet voice within each of us that will not be silenced despite the odds. The storm may rage around us but we want to believe, to dream, to hope. We intend that this collection of words will evoke emotions: passion, enlightenment and hope. And for this hope to be nurtured, to grow, to thrive and to be shared with others.

Sunflowers

Malea Jones

The daisies in my sidewalk
Don't seem to understand
That they should struggle terribly
To grow from stones and sand.
The foot traffic is heavy here,
And kindness must feel rare
But I doubt the daisies in my sidewalk
Can bring themselves to care.
They drink up the dew and sunshine
And smile at everyone they meet
I think we all could learn something
From the daisies near my street.

Peace it Together

Venetia Lagoutaris

Periodically I watch the cars go by,
I watch the people live.
Every now and again someone spares me a smile.
And as they walk by I smile back and wonder,
could everyone smile at me?
Could everyone smile at each other?
For one fleeting second
could the world be nothing more
and nothing less
than me and you
and you and everyone else
smiling?
Every now and again,
someone spares me a smile.

Insignificant?

Tyler Danson

The wind billowed, the waves roared
And beat upon the lonely boat
Carried high upon the swells
As the crew tried to keep her afloat

And hidden deep within her hull
from the tumult of the wind
Near a pivotal point of the bow
A single screw began to bend

The waves beat upon the side
And the ship began to creak
So the tiny screw bent further
And in the height of the storm, grew weak

But the crew never heard it
And the captain paid no mind
For they were busy on the ropes
Lest all the sails unwind

Yet still deep within the hull
Near a pivotal point of the bow
Our single screw began to break
Leaving you to wonder, "how?"

For back at some safe harbor
Where the wind could do no ill
Our little screw was chosen
To bend or break at no one's will

So placed among the many boards
The crew, happy with its make,
Paid it not a moment's notice
not even when it began to break

But the screw alone was fine
As her makers had decreed
Just a little tightening
Was nothing more than it would need

Yet in the height of the storm
While the sails vehemently flapped
This single flaw proved fatal
And our little screw, it snapped

In poured the angry waves
Driven madly by the wind
The boards and plates broke loose
the whole bow began to bend

Once again upon the waves
The life boats now were tossed
But none remembered, for none ever knew
The single screw they lost

Well the captain didn't make it
He went down with the ship
Who sank deep beneath the waves
Caught in Poseidon's grip

The crew cried in agony
While mocked from the ocean floor
By the single screw they'd neglected
A fate to haunt them evermore

So you see, it matters not my son
Whether you're the captain or the crew
You could be the bow itself
Or you could be a single screw

Do not ignore the little things
Ere upon the waves you're tossed
Lest you come to find, as the captain did
That without them we're surely lost

You're Not the Only One

Rey Adieh

I'm just a ghost
but I guess I'm not the only one.
What's the point of going to gym
if I'm always picked last?
I've heard I'm not the only one
but why does it feel like it?

Sitting alone at lunch
Pretending to be on my phone
It's embarrassing
They're staring right at me
Looking right past me
But I guess I'm not the only one.

People start to laugh
People stare past me

You're calling out
I can hear you
We're all in this together
We're gonna make it, if we try

Sometimes it feels like you're on your own
Trust me
You're not the only one . . .

Broken Wings

Becca Jaeger

Hope had fallen
and trust had escaped.
The smiles disappeared
and the loneliness reigned.
The storm had struck
it sent you to this place
where you sit on your knees
with twisted wings of faith.
You were built up
with words and tones.
You were struck down
with words of your own.
There is no cure
for these inevitable things.
There is no cure
for your broken wings.
There is no prevention
for what's happened to life.
There are no more words
to make things right.
You learn to live
like everyone else
you learn to put
your wings on a shelf.
Sometimes you see
other ones fly
attempting to be
or at least to try.
So hope has fallen
but there are still sparks.
Maybe you'll catch one
and ignite your heart.
Belittling words
and broken wings
cannot stop the hero
from stitching the seams.

Stitches

Lauren Donalson

From the moment she wakes
to the moment she takes
her first breath of the day
she feels her body decay.

Like a patchwork doll
her hands and head fall
from their stitches that keep them in place.

She loses a finger
and lets the pain linger.
She loses an eye
her hope says goodbye.

Her body is failing
her mind is wailing
she can't last another night.

As she runs out of thread
to fix what's left of her head
she realizes she's far beyond gone.

She falls to the ground
she can't make a sound
and her body starts fading away.

With her very last breath
which she finds deep in her chest
she whispers a pleading goodbye.

"Someone, help me,
I'm torn too deep.
My thread has run out,

I'm missing my feet."

"My hands fell back there,
and my head is now bare,
someone, help me,
I finally care…"

And as she thought her life was finished
that her living flame had been diminished
she felt a hand, helping her up
a voice saying, "Come on, I'll help you rise up."

She smiled as he lifted her off the ground
and carried her home, got there safe and sound.

He said, "Thank you for calling, I wanted to help,
I was scared by the distance, but I heard your soft mouth."

"You're never alone in this world of torn sewing,
when you run out of thread, I'll help you get going.
No one's life is worth falling apart,
so just ask me for help, and I'll lend you my heart."

Morning

Hannah Rose Nierenhausen

Happiness will seep
through the opening
in your heart
just like the
first rays of sunshine
through the curtains
in the morning.
And it's there
to remind you
to open your arms
and light up the world
because the dark nights
will pass
and the sun will rise.
And so will you.

Song of Spring

Malea Jones

In an instant, the sun had shifted
Through smoke, colors beamed
Rivers once murky red,
Now bubbling crystal streams.

Trampled grass, at once, turned vibrant,
As swords fell to blooming earth.
Arms forgotten, brothers,
No longer blind with hate,
Witnessed rebirth.

Another Good Day

Zan Harris

They dance and they frolic and sing and they play
they stroll to the center of town and they say:
"Another good day, another gold sun!"
"Another fresh morning for work and for fun!"

They work and they toil with neighbors to make
They stroll to the market in town and they spake:
"Another good day, another gold sun!"
"Another hot midday for baking and some!"

They strum and they listen and write and they play
They stroll to the tavern in town and they say:
"Another good round, another good song!"
"Another cool evening relaxing for long!"

They tuck and they doze off and hush and they sleep
They stroll to their homes in the town and they peep:
"Another good day, with much more to come!"
"Another for sisters and brothers and sons!"

They talk and they cheer and discuss and embrace
One another in peace in this small, quiet place.
"We all work as one, without too much fuss."
"I think it'd be nice if more folks were like us."

A Day That Lasts Forever

Julia McQuaig

My eyes are blind to the differences of strangers
The words from my mouth are incapable of malice
The love I feel envelops others with unconditional warmth
Every word that is spoken today is heartfelt

Today we are all of one voice
Today we are all of one heartbeat
Today we celebrate eternal peace

Kindness is the language that we speak
Respect is the guidance for our intentions
The smiles we share are gifts for each other
Violence is a distant shadow that cannot descend

Together, we can make it last forever

For Better

Kalis Figueroa

Smile at your neighbor
Let them know you're there
Help the ones you love
Let them know you care

It often takes so little
An extension of a hand
A mere second of a glance
A glimpse of understanding

Even for a day
Even better for a life
These smallest of things
Could end this world's strife.

Tell Me

Al Hall

You can't tell me
that it is not an issue
When little boys and girls hide under the bed
more afraid of the monsters outside
than anything that could fit in the closet

You can't tell me
that it is not an issue
When babies go to sleep with empty bellies
because both of mommy's jobs aren't enough

You can't tell me
that it is not an issue
When where you come from
determines what you can do

You can't tell me
that it is not an issue
When your daughter sleeps on the street
because you will only accept her as your son

You can't tell me
that it is not an issue
When I watch people in the hall
standing up to laughing peers
because if they don't, no one will

You can't tell me
that all hope is lost
When you can see progress being made every day
by the people who still have
the courage to care

Mr. Glen

Becca Jaeger

"Mr. Glen, tell me a story, tell me how you ended up here."
I had a world
a job in construction
a wife and a little girl.
It all functioned,
until I was caught
in an illegal mess
given a cot
to sleep in prison dress.
When I was made free
I couldn't find a career
no one was a'trusting
the only roof I had was fear.

Even before drifting away from my life
my daughter always hated me
my wife took off in the night.
What I could lose I did, you see?

The world has a funny way of warning
when you begin to steer off track.
If only we rose early in the morning
to catch ourselves veering from the path.
Maybe I wouldn't have lost so much
it was only a little every day
but a little adds up as such
that life makes it end this way.

My daughter is a ghost
she's grown deaf to my voice
so was I to all of life.
In a way, it was my choice.
But I can choose again
to chase after hope,
living like this isn't the end
but a way to cope.

It opened my eyes to feel forgiven
there are people who have learned to care.
So maybe I have felt forsaken
but was I someone who was always there?

I've written to my daughter
gotten in touch with my wife
there are walls separating us farther
and farther away in life
But if you try hard
to knock down those walls
you'll find just how far
you can stand above it all.
Stand tall above the crowd
the lives you've impacted
let those you love hear the sound
you've finally enacted:
your working heart
chasing after your world.
It's a work of art
when you know your little girl
can finally see you;
she sees the glory
in all that you do,
that's the forgiven story.

"Mr. Glen is a story-telling man;
he tells his story of chasing his home.
As he tells me, I begin to understand
life will never leave you alone."